THE PRIDE LIST

EDITED BY SANDIP ROY AND BISHAN SAMADDAR

The Pride List presents works of queer literature to the world. An eclectic collection of books of queer stories, poems, plays, biographies, histories, thoughts, ideas, experiences and explorations, the Pride List does not focus on any specific region, nor on any specific genre, but celebrates the great diversity of LGBTQ+ lives across countries, languages, centuries and identities, with the conviction that queer pride comes from its unabashed expression.

SUDIPTO PAL

Unlove Story

TRANSLATED FROM THE BENGALI BY
ARUNAVA SINHA

LONDON NEW YORK CALCUTTA

Seagull Books, 2024

First published in Bengali as *Bhalo na basar galpo*
by Sristisukh Prakashan, Bagnan, Howrah, India

© Sudipto Pal, 2021

First published in English translation by Seagull Books, 2024

English translation © Arunava Sinha, 2024

The epigraphs to the parts of this volume are quotations from the work of
Rabindranath Tagore, translated from the Bengali by Arunava Sinha.

ISBN   978 1 8030 9 420 5

British Library Cataloguing-in-Publication Data
A catalogue record for this book is available from the British Library

Typeset at Seagull Books, Calcutta, India
Printed and bound by WordsWorth India, New Delhi, India

To Ma, Baba and Biman

BOOK ONE

The Forester

I wander madly around the forest
Driven by own scent, there and here
Like a musk deer.
On the spring night in the southern breeze
I cannot find my way.
What I seek I seek by mistake
What I get I do not seek.

1

'It hurts, Dada.'

'Let it. Make a mistake, get punished.'

Srijan-da was twisting Chikan's ear with one hand while tightly holding on to his young cousin's wrist with the other so that he couldn't escape.

Chikan was my classmate, his formal name was Nachiketa. It was the summer holidays after our Secondary exams. When the caretaker of the mango orchard owned by Chikan's family went home for a few weeks, Chikan's cousin Srijan took charge. Chikan was his assistant, and I went over to lend a hand. Theirs was a joint family—Srijan-da's father was Chikan's uncle; they all lived together under the same roof. Srijan-da, who was studying engineering at the time, had come home for a couple of months between his second and third years at college. I was always keen on gardening, and the skills I picked up during those days came into use many years later. Besides learning, I had another interest—I was drawn more by the forester than by the forest.

In the garden there were more bushes and shrubs than flowers, more toil than pleasure, more fear than joy—fear of Srijan-da. Perhaps my fear was baseless, entirely imagined. But it was amid these mango trees and flowering plants that I arranged my garden and lay in wait—my very own garden that was a mixture of beauty and spirit and fear and anxiety. Anxiety meant anticipation of what tomorrow would bring. And I lived amid these expectations.

There was a great deal of work in the garden—making compost, watering and adding fertilizer, pruning the plants, digging, picking the mangoes, and so much more. I savoured the sight of Srijan-da digging the earth with a crowbar. The late-afternoon sun seemed to be pouring molten gold over him. He worked very hard, and he sweated very hard too. We didn't put in a tenth of the effort that he did. Chikan would get scolded for this. Very often the scolding I deserved was diverted to him, but he would just giggle. So would I. You can't throw your weight around with anyone else like you can with your family. Srijan-da would get it too and chuckle.

'What's so funny, boy?' Srijan-da would ask me.

On certain days, harsher punishment awaited Chikan—such as twisting of ears, just like today. Srijan-da held Chikan's ear with one hand and grabbed his wrist with the other. I looked at the scene and thought, *Why not give me the punishment I deserve, why not hold my hand tightly too?*

Along with the mango trees and flowering plants, there was also a sacred fig tree in the orchard. This tree has leaves of the shape we like to give our hearts. It's like a tree of romance, which spreads love by shedding its leaves. It was beneath such a tree that the Buddha gained nirvana and spread his light among his followers. These thoughts would drift through my mind as I looked at Srijan-da sleeping in the shade of the tree.

This was my only wage for slaving all day. Visual pleasure. The pleasure of gazing not just at the flowers and leaves and vines, but at something else too. At Srijan-da. I'm not the kind who stares wide-eyed at people at any time. So I looked at the man when he slept. As he lay down on the tender grass under the sacred fig tree and the errant breeze blowing over the pond ruffled both the grass and the hair on the sleeping man's chest, I had the urge to say to the wind, *I'm so jealous of you.*

Being shy by nature, I would sit several yards away from where Srijan-da lay, the shade of the tree filling the space between us. The sacred fig tree was not small by any means. But no matter how much distance my timidity insisted I put between him and me, the sheer size of the tree covered this distance with its shade. So I would pray to it to keep the two of us in its shelter all our lives, side by side but with some distance in between.

Srijan-da was strongly built, it was clear that he worked out. He was muscular, but these weren't the rippling muscles that make one appear aggressive and vain about their physical prowess. He would work very hard, so at the end of the day, I'd be tempted to hand him a flower and say, *Here, take this thing you have yourself grown in this garden,* and then sing the song, *'O Forester, may you be reborn as the pining lover Radha'—otherwise how will you know how I ache?*

My reverie would be snapped by Chikan calling us. Such a pest. There I was, dreaming of weaving a garland of love with wildflowers, and that was when he had to bother me. I said, 'Can't you see the man's sleeping after a long day of hard labour? Do you have to bug him right now?'

Chikan would look at me strangely and say, 'The *man*! Oh my god.'

Gazing at Srijan-da wasn't the only reward for working in the garden, there was more. I'd also get what one is supposed to get in a mango orchard—mangoes. Srijan-da taught me how to suck the juice directly without peeling or slicing the fruit. I ended up with more mango juice on my nose, mouth and cheeks than in my stomach.

'Wipe your face, boy.'

But there was no mirror to check whether I had cleaned up properly. So Srijan-da used his eyes and fingers to point out the parts where remnants of mango still lingered. His eyes seemed to scour my face for the slightest trace of mango juice. As if he was a connoisseur of mangoes not ready to spare a single drop of mango juice.

Several creatures' lives were centred around the sacred fig tree—squirrels, woodpeckers, crows, bats, and I. The fig tree was a giant that gave sanctuary to one and all. According to my calculations, it had nearly a hundred thousand leaves. Chikan refused to believe me when I told him this, I had to explain the maths to him. He was so rude! After hearing me out, he said, 'You have nothing but to do these weird sums in your head when you're watching over your precious Srijan-da while he sleeps. You think the bats will carry him off if you don't stand guard?' Such a bastard! Imagine saying Srijan-da is mine!

But he wasn't wrong. I may well have slacked off work and spent my time daydreaming. And when I did so, I would sit beneath the African tulip tree. It stood in a corner of the garden, so it was easy to escape prying eyes there, which I simply had to do, for this was where I would unlock my chest. You shouldn't reveal your treasures to anyone, they will only envy you, suspect you, pester you with questions. I kept my valuables locked away just like grown-ups do. My chest was nothing but my sketchbook, and my treasures were my sketches. In fairy tales, kings stuffed their chests with gems and jewels they had plundered from other kingdoms. I took pride in the fact that I had created my own treasures.

I used to make sketches of the person I liked the most in the garden. After drawing the entire anatomy, I had to cover its nudity with additional strokes. But by then I had learnt how to use these strokes cleverly, how to cover nudity inventively. I used flowers and leaves and fruits, and patted myself on the back, 'This is your own art, your own discovery.'

Sometimes in the inner pages, I left the body uncovered. Thankfully I had not yet learnt how to draw faces accurately, or it would have been so embarrassing to be caught with these sketches. Good boys didn't make such drawings, did they?

Srijan-da didn't boss Chikan alone, he was the boss of the entire orchard. He spotted my sketchbook from a distance. Oh no, he was approaching the African tulip tree now. I was about to tuck the sketchbook in my schoolbag and run, but our eyes met. I was expecting him to grab my wrist like he had Chikan's, and that it would hurt. But he only threw a sidelong glance at me before I escaped.

2

Such a strange dream at night. Srijan-da was genuinely angry and I'd been punished. My ears were smarting. I woke up in a sweat. There was a faint light outside the window. I touched my ears to check—they were fine. We can certainly plead for a dream before we sleep, but we cannot make demands about whether it should be a good dream or a bad one, whether it will come true, whether we will wake up drenched in sweat or with dream-laced eyes.

A chameleon used to hop about in the large flower bushes in the garden. It wasn't visible outside the bush, but you could see it when you parted the leaves and branches. Whenever I caught sight of it, I stared at it intently to see when it would change colour, when it would shed its grey-green attire for a red-orange-yellow one. I had no idea what it stared at all the while, puffing its throat. But it never changed its colour. Reptiles have infinite patience. Seeing me watch the chameleon so intently, Srijan-da would say, 'It won't take on a new colour even if you stare continuously for an hour. It will happen only if it feels colourful, if it's pleased or annoyed by something.'

I had no idea how to please or annoy a chameleon. And I didn't have the patience of one either. Today I looked for it for quite some time too—all by myself. The strange dream kept coming back to me and I continued to examine my ears. Totally distracted, I mixed the compost in incorrect proportions, even cut my finger on a rose thorn. Who knew what calamity lay in wait for me today? Srijan-da was definitely going to beat me up when he saw what I'd been up to. Then I told myself, *No, Srijan-da would never do that. Even though he twisted Chikan's ears, he never laid a finger on me.* But the blood on my finger should have been a warning for me: there's no rose without thorns.

Chikan hadn't shown up that day. Srijan-da complained every day of sore hips and legs because Chikan and I didn't pull our weight. I saw him looking at me from a distance when I was sucking my finger after cutting it on the thorn, but he wasn't in the least bit bothered. There was a touch of contempt in his voice. 'My entire body is in pain after all the work I do and you guys start screaming when you nick your fingers. Your friend's vanished somewhere today, I have no idea where.'

On an impulse I told Srijan-da, 'Let me give you a massage. The aches will go away.'

There was something besides contempt in his eyes, I didn't know what to call it. He looked at me strangely. After a pause, he said, 'OK then, give me a massage. But your finger . . .'

'No worries, it's nothing.'

Srijan-da found a patch of soft grass and lay down on it.

'What's the matter? Get going.'

Was I not supposed to be embarrassed by the way he was gaping at me?

'Lie on your stomach. I'll massage your back.'

'OK.'

I'd observed how barbers give you massages after haircuts. Sometimes they make you sit, other times they make you lie down on a bench. I'd learnt massaging techniques by watching them.

Srijan-da's body quivered as soon as I touched his back with my index finger and thumb. Was it his body or my hand that had trembled? I wasn't sure. But things became normal after this. Out of the blue he asked, 'So, lots of secret drawings?'

'Umm, no . . .'

Suddenly he looked at me. His expression seemed to say that drawing in secret in their garden was a vile act, that I'd committed a crime.

He lowered his eyes again and said very softly, 'You never show me anything you draw.'

'OK, I will.'

'What do you draw though?'

'Mango trees, flowering plants—stuff like that.'

Srijan-da was silent now.

I massaged him carefully, not approaching the front of his body. Shoulders, back, hips, that was all. A ravine ran between two hills on his back, a pair of fingers ran like a slow-moving river through it. The tremors in his body made me think I'd stepped over a line.

He turned over on his back. All this while I wasn't embarrassed because I didn't have to meet his glance. Now, the look in his eyes was thirsty, fervent, as if pleading for a glass of water after a hard day's work. Imagine my superhero Srijan-da gazing at me with pining eyes. Indistinctly he said, 'What is it you want?'

It was so embarrassing. I tried to run away, he grabbed my wrists. I tried to free myself but I wasn't strong enough. Then he said, 'Come.' But where?

There was an outhouse in a corner of the orchard where the caretaker lived. But he was on leave now. So in there we went. He had let go of my hands, but the way I followed him into the outhouse made it seem my wrists were still in his firm grip. You must never ask someone being driven by a dream what binds him to the call of the unknown.

There was nothing really besides a cot in the room. It had neither a mattress nor sheets. Maybe Mr Caretaker had put them away. The plaster was flaking off the walls. A stove stood in a corner. I learnt that the rose gardener does not sleep on rose petals. We sat on the bed. I discovered what it was like to touch Srijan-da's hairy chest. With my hand I tried to feel his thumping heart.

Four years earlier, when I was in Class Seven, I had been to Chikan's house on his sister Mita's ninth birthday. She and her friends were playing doctor and they asked Chikan and me to join. Mita wrote three names on a slip of paper and told me to check their health and give her a report. She handed me a toy stethoscope. The first name was her grandfather's, the second her aunt's and the third—I was seeing the name for the first time in my life—Srijan-da's. I had never set eyes on him before.

Wondering whether to enter his room for the check-up, I was fretting and dying of embarrassment when he looked up from his textbook and beckoned to me with a finger. I approached him fearfully. I must have been looking ridiculous with the toy stethoscope tucked into my ears.

'What's your name, boy?'

'Mallar.'

'And what does that mean?'

'It's a raga.'

'Oh, Megh Mallar—the one they sing in the rainy season, right? So what are you doing in this poor man's room? And why now? It's not raining.'

I didn't know how to answer such peculiar questions.

'Umm Mita said . . .'

'I know, she likes this game. I'm Srijan-da, by the way.'

He added the -da suffix himself to establish he was older. I could have also asked him what his name meant, but I had neither the habit nor the courage to ask so many questions.

I began the check-up with the stethoscope. Even at that early age, Srijan-da already had a well-formed physique and beautiful soft hair on his chest. Holding the stethoscope against his chest through his shirt, I could hear the thumping heart. He looked at me with surprised eyes.

I was trying to listen to the same thumps now, trying to spot the same surprised look in his eyes. But this Srijan-da was not the patient Srijan-da of four years ago. A restless, impatient man, he was expecting something. What's taking you so long? his eyes seemed to be saying.

Things proceeded as in a dream. I'd been to Kolkata a year or so earlier. In a colonial building I'd seen a white marble sculpture in the Greek style. 'Don't touch, they'll scold you,' my mother had said. I didn't know who would scold me. I was touching the sculpture now—and look, no one was scolding me.

My hand went to the navel of the sculpture. Everything was fine until now, my hand was my own, but suddenly it was under his control. For the sculpture was not an inanimate object, it was a living being. He made me unbutton his Bermuda shorts, then guided my hand with his to the spot of pleasure. I tolerated this too. My lips were on his navel, he forced them down to that region. My arena of love was his entire body, but his pleasure was concentrated in that one spot alone. A marble sculpture isn't necessarily a divine figure.

Now I stopped him. I felt someone was forcing me, filling my mouth and tongue and throat with something like a bitter medicine that I didn't want to taste. I moved my mouth away. 'Let me go,' I said.

Can you satisfy the divine forester with only an offering of flowers? Will he be content if you turn yourself into a basket of blooms and serve yourself to him? Or does a god demand something harder from a human? Can such a demand be denied? Can you protest?

How was I to match up to this strength? He tightly held my wrist with his right hand. I wondered whether it hurt Chikan just as much when he gripped his wrist. Then it occurred to me that the two sensations of pain were not the same. I realized that you can at best plead for a dream before going to bed, but you cannot write its screenplay. I didn't know that the nude figure covered with flowers and leaves in my sketchbook would reveal itself in the form of such a monstrous nakedness.

'Don't force me,' I said and shoved him away. He could withstand a shove from me, but I hurt my left shoulder in the scuffle, the tremendous pain from which persisted for a week. An intense pain often mitigates a minor one—the agony in my shoulder made me forget the cut in my finger. I ran away, clutching my shoulder to keep the pain in check. A bewildered Srijan-da still sat stark naked on the floor beside the caretaker's bed.

3

What was it that happened, and why, was it what I had wanted, or was it inevitable—at night in bed I pondered over these things. Some confusing dreams—sometimes I seemed to be fighting relentlessly on a battlefield, sometimes I felt like I was running away, and sometimes, as though I had given up and surrendered. When I woke up I felt I was fine as I was, why fight? Then I reflected, it wasn't exactly a world of love we lived in, and then, maybe I'm not old enough for love.

I didn't go back to the garden. Chikan turned up a couple of days later to find out whether I was OK, Srijan-da himself came over in the afternoon. I packed Chikan off on the pretext of having a cold, but it wasn't so easy getting rid of his older cousin.

I was in the veranda, practising sketching. You need a subject if you want to sketch, but I could find neither a subject nor a theme. Flowers, trees, vines, leaves, people—I had decided not to draw anything I'd seen in the orchard. Sitting absent-mindedly with a 2B pencil on the sketchbook in my lap and an HB pencil held between my teeth, I gazed at the sky and the road alternately as though a subject would fly in or walk up to present itself. All of a sudden, I saw a familiar figure coming my way. On a motorbike.

'Want to go get a chicken roll, Mallar?' As though nothing had happened.

'We're going out in a bit, why don't you go get one.'

'Hmm.'

After lunch during the summer holidays, when there was absolutely nothing to do, flipping aimlessly through magazines became an important task. I wasn't allowed to read these magazines as a child, they were locked away in bookcases. Apparently they were for grown-ups, that too meant only for women. But now I was considered a grown-up, so the magazines were kept within my reach. Ever since childhood, I had assumed they had racy pictures, but now I was disappointed to see they contained nothing but fashion, recipes and medical advice. So much for magazines meant for grown-ups!

In the section on mythology, I found a psychological analysis of why in the Mahabharata Kunti couldn't reject the Sun god's plea to offer herself to him. Then in the advice section, I found someone asking, 'What kind of husband should women choose?' How many women in our country get to choose their husbands, I wondered, and even if they do, how big is the choice to begin with? An expert on relationships had answered, 'Don't marry anyone who spends his day on nothing but his nine-to-five job. Marry someone who knows how to cook things from all over the world, or paints, or plays an instrument, or gardens, etc., etc. . . . .'

I shut the magazine. No, I didn't want someone who gardens.

He came again the next day. I wasn't in the veranda, he got my mother to fetch me.

'Want to go get some moglai parota?'

I might be crazy about eating chicken rolls and moglai parotas, I said in my head, *but I'm not a kid whom you can placate this way.*

On the third day, I sat in the veranda, most likely deliberately. I wanted to see what he would tempt me with today.

'Hey Mallar, do you like this watch of Srijan-da's?'

'Don't know.'

'You said your parents would give you a watch if you ace your Secondary exams.'

'So?'

'That's some way off. Why don't you keep this one for the time being? No, never mind, this one's old, I'll give you another one like this.'

'Don't want.'

'But you used to like Srijan-da's watch.'

I knew why he said this. One day he'd been swimming in the pond, having left his clothes and watch beneath the tree. Out of sight behind the tree trunk, I had run my hands over them. And I was caught in the act. But I had picked up the watch not simply because it was a watch but because it was Srijan-da's. As though even the watch held the scent of his body . . . but never mind all that.

'No, I didn't. Go now.'

As he turned to go back, I called out to him on an impulse.

'Srijan-da!'

I didn't know what it was that I could expect from this relationship. Like the little child who picks seashells on the shore, looking inside each of them for a pearl, or is simply content with shells of various colours, I too was gathering anything that lay in front of me on the assumption it was eternal and unfading—whether it was happiness or sorrow, love or unlove, humiliation or something else. Sixteen-year-olds don't apply reason to their thoughts.

But why so much effort to please me? Was he afraid I might accuse him of harassing an underage boy? Whom would I complain to anyway? It would mean trouble for both of us—I was involved too.

'Don't want your watch,' I said. 'Can I ask for something else?'

'What?'

'Take me to Kali Dighi.'

You should take advantage of a man with a motorbike. Kali Dighi was an hour away, not an easy journey. I couldn't get there on my bicycle. I didn't know if it was shameless of me, perhaps I was forgiving him even before he had asked for forgiveness. I was lightening the burden of his guilt before anyone got to know of it. I knew I wasn't thinking rationally, but in the absence of any other driver, being driven by my dreams seemed useful.

Looking up at the sky, Srijan-da scratched his head and then his chin, and finally said, 'The clouds look like . . .' and continued after a pause, 'a thunderstorm.'

Was this a ruse to turn me down? Then he looked at me and said with a devilish smile, 'What? Why do you look so sad?'

'Umm no . . .'

'Let's go then.'

Switching on the engine, he said, 'It'll be dark soon, we won't have too much time there.'

'No problem.'

'What'll you tell your mother?'

'That's for me to figure out.'

My mother would have killed herself worrying if I'd gone with someone else, but Srijan-da had a reputation in the neighbourhood—respectable family, student of engineering, blah blah blah.

Kali Dighi was pretty far by any standards. Nowadays, even this semi-rural town of ours had become a concrete jungle, but at Kali Dighi you could still see a long way into the distance. A mysterious body of water, soothing darkness, faint lights dancing on the surface. Next to it was a temple to Shiva and Kali, which used to send shivers down my spine when I was a child. There was a giant banyan tree too, beneath which a madman would always be waiting for someone to arrive. I was more frightened of him than of Goddess Kali.

'It's a long way, let me get you a helmet too,' Srijan-da said. 'Wait at the end of the lane, I'll fetch another helmet from my place. If I take you home, Chiku will ask a thousand questions and want to come along too.'

This gave me quite a thrill. I didn't know Srijan-da particularly well before I started working in the garden. Just as well. People you know from childhood feel like they're family, as if they're your own siblings. But now it seemed as if Srijan-da and I were off on a secret tryst and Chikan was trying to prevent us, just as Radha's mother-in-law and sister-in-law tried to ensure she didn't sneak off to meet Krishna. I felt quite grown up, but then the very next moment I realized this was neither a romance nor an assignation. In fact, I had no idea what it was.

But why was it taking him so long to bring a helmet? Then I saw he'd swapped his grey T-shirt for a red shirt. He read my expression correctly. 'Now what are you tense about?'

I felt the mild pain in my shoulder while getting on the motorbike, but I wasn't going to care much about it now, for that would mean being stuck at home. You must try to get your joy through your pain, or it hurts even more.

Sunset was not far off by the time we got to Kali Dighi. The noisy rituals in the temple ended soon afterwards. The madman beneath the banyan tree was singing, *You've cast your net all over the world—are you a fisherman's daughter, Kali?*

There were electric lights everywhere on the northern side of the lake. We moved away from the light pollution. The enchanting silence was slowly turning into the deafening chirping of crickets. We found a rock and sat down on it. The electric lights didn't cast much of a glow here, the only illumination came from a half-moon and the faint stars. A light in which you could see each other's eyes, but not read everything in them.

By that light I saw Srijan-da trying to say something.

'The other day I thought you wanted it too. But . . .'

He looked into my eyes for an answer to his incomplete question. But the light here didn't reveal everything. I didn't respond, and I didn't let my eyes do it either, turning them away towards the lustrous darkness of the water. Since he hadn't got an answer from my eyes, let him look for it in my silence.

Some time passed. I began to wonder why I'd wanted to come here in the first place. He was about to get to his feet, perhaps he found such a long wait for an answer intolerable. But I didn't want it to end just yet. I took his hand as he stood up. He turned back towards me. I tugged at his hand to make him sit down again. He freed his hand after a while.

I had already felt his touch even before what took place the other day. When he was teaching me how to suck the juice out of a mango without peeling it, and I was struggling with the mango pulp smeared all over my face, he had once picked up a drop of juice next to my lips with his fingertip and put it in his mouth. When I was afraid to try and swim in the pond, he spared no effort to convince me. I went down the steps leading to the water, one, two, three—I was wondering whether to go further when I found the finely built and unclothed man beckoning at me. The call of the body helped me ignore my trepidation and approach the water before fear overtook me again. Now he was drawing me by the hand to the middle of the pond. I was gaining courage, but he was too smart—he let my hand go mid-pond. I was about to tumble into the water, but he held me upright.

There was no counting the number of times he had made me go under in this way. Not that he did it with great care each time, sometimes he would just drag me in by the hand or leg, or grab me from the back and push me in. I never disliked those touches.

Now he squeezed my hand gently before freeing himself and said, 'Too many mosquitoes, let's walk around a bit.'

So strange! When I tried touching him, he wouldn't give in. And when he tried to force me like a threatening beast, I refused to surrender. And when I did submit to him, he concealed the beast within himself—such double standards. Was he taking care to avoid my touch? How was I to explain to him the kind of touch I liked and the kind I didn't?

'You're a little boy, Mallar—see, I'm so much older.'

You didn't think I was a little boy the other day, I thought. I was simultaneously a boy of sixteen and a grown-up of sixteen to everyone in the world. His stiffness made me realize he did want to touch me again, but perhaps there was some fear.

'Let's go. This darkness is getting to me. Best to go back now,' I said.

On the way back, the same thought occurred to me—I didn't know what I'd been expecting.

4

There was a summons from the zamindar house. I didn't know whether Srijan-da's ancestors were feudal landlords or not, but the house was enormous, the prayer room and staircase had marble floors, broad pillars ascended to a high ceiling in front of the portico, stained-glass arches sat above doors and windows, the beds were of teak, bronze busts were scattered all around, and, of course, there was the orchard. So everyone called it the zamindar house.

Srijan-da's third-year classes were about to start, he was leaving. Our Class Eleven had begun too. My mother told me about the summons as soon as I came home from school. I left at once on my cycle. She called me from the back, 'Eat before you go . . . change out of your school uniform . . . why are you taking your schoolbag . . .' Who was listening?

When I arrived, I was told to go to Srijan-da's room. Each of them in the family had a room to themselves. I'd been to Chikan's room many times, but this was only my second time in Srijan-da's room, after the first visit four years ago.

A clock as tall as a human being stood beneath the staircase. Zamindars used to live here after all. The pendulum and dial were placed behind sheets of glass set into a wooden frame. I used the dim reflection of my face in the glass to fix my hair. I hadn't combed it before leaving home, and I didn't want to look dishevelled when I met Srijan-da.

Reflected in the same glass I saw the figure of Chikan at a distance, walking away. How odd of him to go away without coming up to me. Anyway, not my problem. I went off to the room where my presence had been sought.

Srijan-da was packing. I was doing what I'd come for, which meant watching him. So many shoes—my God—and so many bottles of deodorant and cologne on his shelves. He had told me once that whatever he earned from coaching students near his college was spent on shoes and fragrances. I tried the colognes and deodorants, which made me realize why I was drawn by the way this man smelt.

Looking very busy, Srijan-da said, 'It's all mixed up now, the laundered clothes and the dirty ones.'

'Let me sniff them and tell you which ones are washed and which are not.'

'Naughty boy—you'll get one tight slap,' said Srijan-da playfully.

'What did I say?'

'Never mind, I know what you're up to.'

So sniffing clothes was an indecent thing to do.

'Like this cologne?'

'I do.'

'I like it a lot too. A whiff of timber with a touch of grapes.'

I had no idea whether it smelt of wood or grapes. All I knew was it smelt exactly like Srijan-da.

'Keep it,' he said.

'No way, I'm an ordinary guy, I'm not into this stuff.'

'You can tell your mother Srijan gave it to you for pruning the rose bushes in their garden.'

'Fine.'

'And what have you got in your schoolbag?'

I took a notebook from my bag and held it out to him. There was a large envelope inside. Srijan-da looked at it for some time.

'Open it.'

What emerged was a sketch.

'It's for you,' I said.

There was a smile in Srijan-da's eyes, and an effort to hide it on his lips.

'So who's the guy sleeping beneath the tree?'

'As if you don't know him.'

'OK. And who's the boy keeping guard?'

'Very funny, stop now.'

'But there's something you forgot.'

'Like what?'

'The artist must sign at the bottom of the sketch.'

'Give it to me, I'll sign.'

'The date must be added too.'

I scribbled it: 1st of July.

'Add the year.'

'Maybe that's something you can just try and remember.'

In my head I said, *I'm sure You'll jot this year down in your mental notebook, it's not like any other year.*

'Got it! So this was what someone was drawing in the garden and hiding from me.'

'Hmm.'

'And running away every time he saw Srijan-da.'

Some time went by watching Srijan-da scratch his head and arrange things in his suitcase.

'Not disturbing your packing, am I?'

'Not at all, the moral support is most welcome,' sniggered Srijan-da.

'Now I will.'

'What?'

'Disturb you.'

I was sitting on a desk. Getting off, I mustered my courage and stood looking into his eyes. I didn't know how I'd grown bold enough to lock eyes with him. Srijan-da was clearly uncomfortable, his eyes darting this way and that as he bit his lips and tongue and turned his face away. On some impulse, he kissed my forehead and said, 'You're a sweet boy, Mallar—just be calm, OK?'

This time I planted a kiss on his lips.

'What are you doing? The door's open.'

'I locked it.'

'What a devil,' Srijan-da said in surprise, 'you're really smart, aren't you?'

Now I flung myself at him, trying to suck out everything from his lips with mine. I was out of control. With great effort, he calmed me down. 'Listen to me, Mallar. Srijan-da isn't running away, I'll be back.'

Who was listening?

Grabbing me and carefully putting me back on the desk, he said, 'Listen to me, baby, you're so young, I even have to make you sit on the desk to talk face to face. Grow up a little more before . . .'

Even in my frenzy, this made me laugh. Should I grow an inch every year over the next few years, I doubted if I'd be tall enough to stand eye to eye with this six-foot man.

When I had quietened down a bit, he said, 'Enough for today, keep the rest for when we meet again.'

I was hurting. The only consolation was what he'd said 'when we meet again' and 'not running away'. Perhaps we'd meet again, but how to placate myself with this hope? I left his room in anger, wiping my eyes, negotiating the staircase somehow with my schoolbag. I felt like I was going to slip on those marble stairs and fall. I couldn't balance on the cycle either, I walked home with it, taking a circuitous route around the pond by the palm trees to ensure the neighbours didn't see my red eyes.

Keeping my voice as normal as possible and averting my eyes, I gave my mother the excuse of homework and locked myself in my room. From my geometry box, I extracted the compass and divider, hoping to distract myself with doodles.

'Have your food,' my mother called from the other side of the door.

'Not hungry, Ma.'

'What's wrong, are you sick? Your eyes looked red.'

'No, I ate over there. Doing my homework now.'

I regretted leaving the way I did. I didn't even take the cologne Srijan-da had given me so lovingly. I'd have felt better holding it now.

All kinds of rubbish was running through my head when there was another knock on the door.

'Not hungry, Ma. Have to finish homework.'

'No, there's something else I want to talk about. Open the door.'

'In a bit.'

Five minutes later, I unlocked the door and went up to my mother in the drawing room. Handing me something wrapped in a piece of cloth like a handkerchief, she said, 'That whatshis-name of yours had come, he left this for you. I asked him to have a cup of tea, he said he had a train to catch.'

I rushed back to my room without hearing her out, locked the door and began to unwrap the package. What was with all these tight knots? In my haste I ended up making them tighter. Eventually, I undid the knots and what emerged was a familiar man—no, not the man, but the smell of that familiar body. The cologne.

5

'Keep the rest for when we meet again,' Srijan-da had said. The words kept ringing in my ears, *when we meet again*. But the cuckoos had arrived and cried spring and gone back two times while I waited for that day. He came back two years later, after spending the summer in between in Chennai on an internship. He had been to his house once, but I was visiting my grandparents on my mother's side at the time. Now I had a break after my Higher Secondary exams. The summons came once again from the zamindar residence.

I had already found out that he was back. On my way to buy groceries in the morning, I'd spotted a set of familiar clothes hung up to dry on their terrace. I'd laughed to myself when I saw them, *So this is what you do, you look out for these signs.*

Checking my reflection on the face of the clock, I fixed my hair and went upstairs.

'You've grown up—a lot!'

'What's with the moustache?' was the first thing I asked him.

'You don't like it?'

'It's nice, but it would be nicer if it wasn't there.'

'Shave it off then.'

I enjoyed myself being a barber, I was having fun. And this man was so naughty, he kept taking the foam off his face and dabbing it on my nose and cheeks.

'I'll shave your nose off along with the moustache if you don't behave yourself.'

'I'd better protect my nose. I'm quite scared of this guy.'

Looking closely at the subtlest of creases on his face with the razor in my hand, I wanted to say a lot of things. Say, *I've saved the bottle of cologne after using half of it*. Say, *That was the only memory you left me*. But the poetry was all inside me, it never made it to my tongue. All I managed to ask after summoning a bit of courage was, 'Were you waiting?'

'Of course I was. You have to wait for the barber when your beard grows too long, don't you?'

This wasn't the answer I wanted, but it wasn't unexpected either. Srijan-da gazed at me for a while. Then he spoke again. 'Do you want a different reply?'

'Who knows?'

'Tell me.'

'Never mind.'

When I was done, I said, 'Time to pay the barber, sir. Not taking less than fifty, sir.'

'You'll get it. Want to work in the garden?'

That garden was my ruination, I muttered silently. What I told him was, 'The caretaker is not on leave.'

'No, this time we'll grow a garden on the roof. A flower garden. Chrysanthemums, dahlias, orchids. Want to?'

He had set a condition before setting up the garden. I'd thought it wouldn't be difficult. But difficult or easy, there was no way to say no.

This time we had decided the garden would be grown with our own money. The funding would come from Srijan-da's internship salary and my earnings from tutoring schoolchildren. Chikan wasn't particularly interested in the garden last time, and even less so this time. So it was just the two of us.

We decided to pick our seeds only from the best nurseries. The advantage was that this meant travelling long distances, which in turn meant going to various places on Srijan-da's motorbike. I rode pillion and sometimes I got to hug him from the back.

Not just seeds, we went around to buy pots too. We got some of the beautifully decorated ones that gypsy women sold by the road. Later, though, we bought plain pots that I hand-painted. I made all kinds of weird art on them—Warli paintings, hieroglyph-like symbols, figures of Ganesh. I enjoyed this more than gardening. This was how our rooftop garden grew.

'Chikan doesn't help at all, and you're busy painting the pots.'

Chikan wasn't even supposed to be there. Paying no attention to Srijan-da's complaint, I said, 'Can I paint a sun on your hand? And a sailboat?'

'You poked me with your pen many times yesterday, do you think it doesn't hurt Srijan-da?'

'Not a pen, I have watercolours, look.'

'Do I have a choice, Michelangelo? Go for it. What if the colour doesn't come off?'

'Watercolours are never permanent. They'll be washed off with your bath tomorrow. I can soap them off if you like.'

'Shameless guy,' chuckled Srijan-da. 'I can't deal with this— is there no end to your demands? Now he wants to soap off the colours.'

'Let me paint first, OK?'

'All right, but not the sun and a sailboat. Do you think my arm is your art-class notebook? Paint something else.'

I took a good look at Srijan-da. Then with my brush I wound grapevines around his arms, corresponding to his muscles. I made a pair of flowers. Looking at his painted hand it suddenly occurred to me that two years ago I had to draw flowers, vines and leaves to cover the torso I had sketched, and today I had painted flowers and vines with my brush on that same flesh-and-blood body.

'Remember the condition we agreed to, Mallar?'

'I remember perfectly. Don't jump, I'm not done yet.'

'What if the colours don't come off?'

'My job was to paint, I've done it. Getting the colours off is your job.'

'So rude.'

'If the colours don't come off when you bathe, wait for the first rain. I will take you myself to get drenched in it.'

One day the rain did come. I dragged Srijan-da off to the field to get wet.

'How about some radha-bollobhi in the rain?' he asked—just the right snack, aptly named after Radha's divine lover, the forester.

'Let's go!'

The grace of monsoon doesn't yield itself to the eyes and ears as much as it does to the nose. The aroma of heeng-laced radha-bollobhi being fried in oil blended with the petrichor. I was trying to inhale this smell from the handwoven plate of leaves on which our food had been served when I found Srijan-da grinning at me.

'What's so funny?'

'You seem to be eating with your nose. So.'

'Oh really?'

'Open your mouth.'

Srijan-da wrapped a piece radhabollobhi around a chunk of curried potato that came with it and popped it into my mouth.

Our celebration of the first day of the rains was going quite well, but unexpectedly Srijan-da chose to ask, 'Chiku and you don't talk any more, have you fought?'

Of course you had to ask me this lousy question just as these smells were making me feel good, I thought. *Can't you stand seeing me happy?*

'All right, don't answer if you don't want to.'

'No, you might as well listen. Since you've given me a chance, I'm going to tell you.'

I began the story. This was about a year and a half ago. I didn't remember when and how Chikan and I stopped talking to each other as much as we used to, perhaps I didn't notice. In Class Eleven, we went to school less often anyway. We were forbidden to dress up in school, but coaching classes were a different matter. Many of the boys wore stylish clothes and gelled their hair to catch the attention of the girls. I didn't do any of this, but one day I went to the English class wearing cologne. Chikan was seated behind me. In a low voice he asked, 'So much cologne? Who've you got your eyes on?'

'No one, just like that.'

'Please, that's enough. I know very well who you got this cologne from. I know the fragrance.'

'Oh really?'

'This is what boys like you do.'

'Boys like me? What do you mean? Do what?'

'Please others. And get colognes for themselves.'

I didn't reply. He continued, 'I never imagined boys like you would do these things too. I know everything.'

I had been told harsh things ever since childhood and was thick-skinned by now. But what upset me most was that someone whom I considered my closest friend, who once protected me from bullies, was now abusing me to my face.

But not even silence can ensure that arguments are avoided. I was some distance from the coaching class when Chikan came up to me from the back and started again.

'If I'd known earlier . . .'

'What if you had? You'd make sure I didn't meet your Dadabhai, your older brother?'

'Dadabhai is not like you.'

'Go ask your Dadabhai yourself.'

Now he backed off on his own. The next day I found people whispering about me in school. I told Chikan, 'It wasn't a ghost that brought me the cologne. Nor did it fly from your house to mine. It came from someone in your family.'

This worked to an extent. I managed to get through the remaining year and a half of my school life.

I stopped and looked at Srijan-da. Perhaps he hadn't realized I was expecting a response, he got it a moment later. 'Chiku wasn't right to do this,' he said. 'I'll talk to him, I'll tell him he can't do this.'

No matter how much Srijan-da scolded Chikan for making mistakes in the garden, I doubted very much that he would say anything to him for my sake, or take the problem home for that matter. I only had his verbal assurance to go by, I didn't hope for anything more.

The rain had let up. I came out of the shop and into the field beyond, letting the gentle raindrops caress me.

Srijan-da stepped out too and said, 'It hurts a lot, doesn't it, Mallar?'

I didn't answer.

'Are you hiding your tears behind the raindrops? Boys tend to.'

'No.'

'If giving me a hug makes you feel better, come.'

I thought of telling him, *Yes, I like hugging you, and if I hug you it's because I like hugging you. Don't imagine I'm seeking shelter with you.*

6

I was stopped suddenly as I was cycling. The gentleman had popped up from nowhere and was tightly holding the handle of my bicycle.

'So where's someone off to? And why didn't someone come to work today?'

'I told you yesterday I was taking the day off.'

'So?' Srijan-da had practically forced my cycle from the main road into a lane. 'Where are you going?'

'Not going anywhere, I'm on my way back.'

'From?'

'The temple.'

'Never known you to be religious.'

'Ma and Baba took me.'

'And where are they?'

'They took a rickshaw home.'

'I'm sure they won't be too worried to know their son's been kidnapped on the way back.' Srijan-da guided my cycle across the bumpy road towards his family orchard. 'So what was the occasion?'

'Seems to me you know everything.'

'And why didn't someone tell me it's his birthday?'

'Just like that.'

'Just like that? And what did your mother say at the temple? The boy's grown up quite a bit, O Lord Shiva, now if I could only dump this sack of potatoes on someone I'd be relieved—is that what she prayed for?'

'Don't know.'

'So how old is someone now?'

'Eighteen.'

'That's right! But why did someone go red when revealing their age?'

This was true, I was wondering myself why I was embarrassed to tell him how old I was. I was still lurching from one side to the other as he dragged me across the rough terrain.

'So how did you find out?'

'Your friend, your enemy, Chiku. He told me sarcastically this morning, *Is this patient waiting for the gardening partner? It's his birthday.* Chikan uses the impersonal passive voice for everything these days.'

'So why did he go out of his way to tell you? He must have caught on that you were waiting for me—am I right?'

'Shouldn't I wait just because you took the day off?'

'I see. And how did you know the route I'd be taking?'

'Srijan-da knows everything. The rooftop is high up, my boy, you can see everything from there.'

'No, only when you're looking out for someone.'

'And so I was.'

'So is the wait over?'

'Of course. You're eighteen now.'

Srijan-da came to an abrupt halt. He was still clutching the handle of my cycle and looking at me with confident yet playful eyes.

'Need to go home, Ma's waiting,' I said.

'Shh! Come to the orchard, we have to pick mangoes.'

'It'll rain any moment, look at the sky.'

'Want to be beaten up? You don't have a choice, Srijan-da is taking you around the orchard.'

Everything between us began in this orchard, but for some reason I didn't particularly want to go back there. We wandered around idly for some time. Srijan-da was trying to whistle a tune. He wasn't quite getting it, but I figured out the Tagore song. *The forest's song / hasn't ended yet, it goes on / must you at once disappear / just as the buds are here / in my forest of jasmines . . .* Was that the one? As we walked, Srijan-da kept nudging my elbow with his or planting his foot on mine. He seemed intent on irritating me. When I turned towards him, he looked away, whistling.

The clouds gathered in an instant, and the rain began. The outhouse gave us sanctuary. Shibu-da, the caretaker, seemed quite pleased to see us.

'Sit down, let me make some tea.'

We sat. There was just the one place to sit. The bed now had a mattress and sheets, but other than that, the room was the way it had been two years ago.

'Is everything OK, Mallar?' Srijan-da asked in a low voice.

'Don't know.'

I went out of the room and sat on the floor beneath the temporary roof protruding overhead.

'Can I ask you something, baby?'

'Don't.'

'I know why you don't like this place. How did you forgive the person responsible for the incident when you can't forgive the place where it happened?'

'Have I forgiven? I don't exactly know what forgiving means.'

Srijan-da looked at me without any expression. I continued, 'I constantly keep in mind the condition you'd set. It makes my days go well. No need to think of anything else.'

'I'm bringing your tea outside.' Shibu-da appeared with three tumblers of tea.

7

Most days I avoided Chikan when going up to the roof, even though he'd resumed talking to me now and then on his own. Either Srijan-da had kept his word and spoken to his cousin, or Chikan had more or less realized he'd have to tolerate my presence on the roof of their house throughout the summer holidays. I never tried to find out which of these was the real reason.

I went to their house twice a day, morning and afternoon, to do the gardening and paint the pots. I had just gone up to the roof that morning like I did every day when I discovered a smartly dressed Chikan coming downstairs. He was looking happy until then, but on spotting me he made his expression glum. 'My cousin's getting married, we're on our way there. We've been invited for all the meals.'

I was about to speak, but Chikan already knew what I'd say. Sarcastically he quipped, 'Not to worry, your Srijan-da isn't going. Everyone else is. Dadabhai will go in the evening.'

I continued up to the roof. When you consider someone your hero, your ideal, you're bound to be disillusioned if they turn out to be different from the image you've built in your head. And it's all the more annoying when the reason for the disillusionment is right in front of your eyes. So I got why Chikan was irritated. And it probably even gave me a little pleasure.

'How come you didn't go?'

'I get bored there, I'll go in the evening.'

Srijan-da turned the soil over in the pots while I painted a pot. This had become my passion, and if it turned out particularly well I didn't allow the pot to be dirtied with soil and plants—I put it on display with the other pots. Srijan-da teased me about this, always threatening to use my pots for his plants.

I was running my paintbrush across a pot when Srijan-da blinked at me.

'So Michelangelo has become a potter now.'

'So it seems.'

'But there's extra work today, baby. You'll have to work overtime.'

'Oh really?'

'Can't go home for lunch.'

'I haven't told Ma.'

'The cook's going out on an errand, I've told him to inform your mother.'

'All right then. You're all sweaty, go have a bath.'

Taking off all his clothes except his drawers, Srijan-da said, 'I'd better go downstairs now.'

'Why do you need to go downstairs?'

'Where will I have a bath then?'

'Right here.'

'Here?'

Before he knew, I'd picked up the hosepipe used to water the plants.

'Behave yourself, or you'll get a thrashing.'

But he was drenched before he could do anything. Now he was charging at me.

'Come on, give me that hosepipe.'

'Don't drench me, how will I go home?'

'Not my problem.'

I ran into the solitary room on the roof.

Inside, there was a grandfather clock, very old, as tall as a human, quite lovely. It had been dumped here because it no longer worked. It was about to topple and break when I dashed into it, I managed to stop the fall with my hand.

'That's an antique piece, there's a fine for breaking it.'

'How much?'

'Come closer and I'll show you how much.'

We spent the rest of the day in the room on the roof, improvising with odds and ends piled up in there. There was an old trunk packed with clothes. At Srijan-da's bidding, I pulled out an old sheet with floral patterns and spread it on an old mattress—it became our wedding bed of flowers.

Spent, the man eventually went off to sleep. I watched him snore, his naked, hairy chest rising and falling with his breath—it rose, fell, swelled, shrank. Six years ago I had checked his breathing with a toy stethoscope, today I was doing it with my eyes.

It was quite warm despite its being a rain-drenched day. Poking around in the room, I found an ancient table fan. An electrical socket too, to plug it in. The blades were covered in soot and dust. Srijan-da's singlet was dry, I used it to wipe the blade. Hopefully I wouldn't be scolded for this. I moved the fan next to the mattress, pointed it at Srijan-da, and turned it on. But all that happened was that he woke up at the clatter.

'I just thought you might be feeling hot.'

'Good move. Let me sleep some more.'

Ten minutes later, he said in a sleep-laced voice, 'You didn't have hair on your chest before, baby.'

'I'm two years older, sir. Don't you like it?'

'I like it very much. Haven't you seen me sleeping in the orchard? Who doesn't like soft tender grass to lie on?'

Srijan-da came closer. Burying his nose in my chest, he said, 'I was scared, you know, what if you pushed me away again?'

'I didn't like it that day. Today . . .'

'Today?'

'Who knows?'

He asked a single question before he resumed snoring.

'You do remember what you promised?'

'I do.'

The man opted for another round of sleep. When we woke up, he began to laugh at me.

'What's this you've done?'

'Why, what's wrong with it?'

I'd been downstairs to get him a fresh shirt and pair of shorts and placed them neatly next to the mattress.

'You've laid out my clothes.'

'My mother had given my sister tips for married life—always neatly lay out your husband's clothes, handkerchiefs and socks for him.'

'Am I your husband or what?'

Silently, I thought, *Not husband, you're a hunter, you'll vanish after making your kill.*

8

'Is this any way to wake someone up, you rascal?'

I bit off a single small strand of his beard. Poor thing, it must have hurt. But I couldn't find any other way to wake him up at that moment.

'I heard the phone ring many times downstairs. Go answer it,' I said. Far from answering the phone, he drew me down to the mattress again.

It was evening in no time. I could hear the strains of the shehnai in the distance. Several weddings were probably being held nearby. If a melancholic strain from the shehnai blew in from one direction, there was joyous percussion from another.

Gathering the rose petals that Srijan-da had brought in from the roof garden and scattered on me, I pressed them one by one between the pages of my sketchbook and said, 'It's evening, the phone's been ringing non-stop, let's go downstairs now.'

Srijan-da's mother had called several times from the wedding venue.

'The groom's family is about to arrive . . . they're serving dinner to the first batch of guests . . . when are you getting here?'

'Getting ready, Ma.'

I'd scrubbed his face with lemon and put a pack on it ten minutes earlier.

'I'll take the help of this magazine for the dhuti.' Neither of us knew how to put one on.

'Ah, he's over the moon at getting this chance. Naughty boy!'

Helping him dress up in a dhuti and a panjabi, I sprayed cologne on him and said, 'Not this leather band, put on your father's gold watch with the silver strap.'

After I'd got him ready, I mused, *Are you my very own creation, Srijan? No one but a poet could have created those eyes like poetry. This beauty is no less than an artist's imagination. And is there another poet and artist in this village besides me?* And then I reflected, *No, you're even more beautiful than my imagination. The creator who has brought poetry, melody, rhythm and music into the world must have combined all of them to create you.*

'Enough, let me leave now,' said Srijan-da. 'Ma will kill me if I'm late.'

Slipping a pair of nagra shoes on his feet, I said, 'One day you'll get married, and on that day I'll dress you up just like this. You'll look beautiful. You'll invite me, won't you?'

Let me go back a few weeks, when the work on the garden was yet to begin, and talk about the condition we had agreed to. Not exactly a condition—rather, one could call it our Constitution. If the garden we were creating was a small country, this was its rule book. Let me narrate what happened the day it was drawn up.

'I'm not in love with you,' said Srijan-da. 'And I won't be.'

I gazed at him.

'You won't fall in love with me either,' he continued. 'Being in love with each other—that's one thing neither of us will do. Can you nurture this garden without loving me?'

I kept gazing at him.

'That's the condition. Can you do it?' he repeated.

I agreed.

I didn't know at that time how not to love. I had to learn it slowly. Making a pledge of love when circling the fire seven times at your wedding and then keeping the pledge is difficult enough. But the pledge not to love isn't easy either. You don't have to remind yourself every morning of the promise to love. Love happens on its own, or not at all. But you have to remind yourself every day of the vow *not* to love, you have to keep it in your head all the time through everything you do.

But even when we didn't love, we might have knowingly or unknowingly given each other some love in various ways—one of us less, the other one more. Many years later, Srijan-da's father told him, 'I can't look after these flowers of yours any more, you people live so far away now. Most of the plants have dried up—should I get rid of them?' I learnt later that he had replied, 'Throw away the plants but send the hand-painted pots to me in Chennai. Make sure to get the best packer so they don't break. Don't worry about the expenses, I'll pay.'

BOOK TWO

Dream Wanderer

Forever distant, like a stranger
In a strange and private land,
You come close and yet not near,
You go back—why do you keep going back
Bearing a thwarted desire?

1

'You're getting married, I heard?'

I was drawing patterns on the sand on the Mahabalipuram beach, alternately with my fingers and toes. The tide, or someone else's footprints, would wipe these out in a while. Let them. I was happy just to draw. Not all traces can be preserved, nor should they remain. There are many things that are not meant to endure.

I was meeting Srijan-da after five years. There had been no contact in between. After the holidays following my Higher Secondary examination, we had walked our separate paths—I with my higher education, he with his job. I'd only get news of him sometimes from my family.

Srijan-da didn't answer my question.

'See, Mallar, one of the problems in our lives—I mean not just yours and mine—is that when two people talk, they talk less and less about each other and more and more about others.'

'That's true.'

'We'll talk only about you and me these two days. There are enough people to talk about others. Are you up for it?'

'OK.'

'You know what our other problem is? We talk more about the past and the future than about the present.'

'Right.'

'We won't talk of yesterday and tomorrow. Only of today—all right?'

'All right.'

'So what do we have here? We'll have the first and second persons, no third person. We'll have the present tense, no past or future tense.'

I know of grammar when it comes to language, but sometimes we have to impose a grammar or some rules on our subjects and statements and thoughts, or else they fly out of our reach. Everyone loves to fly, but Srijan-da wanted the winged horse to be reined in a bit. He made me accept a condition every time. I had no resentment about them. I'd got what I wanted, perhaps precisely because of these conditions. During this meeting after five years, we might as well not reminisce about what we did five years ago, or what we did during the past five years.

'Let me see what you've drawn on the sand, baby.'

I hadn't drawn anything really, and whatever little there had been was now covered by the foam from the sea. It wasn't as though everything had to be drawn on paper and encased in frames. Sometimes I had an impulse to sketch on the sand for the sea to erase at its whim.

This was what happened about four days ago. I was in Chennai for a couple of weeks for work. I don't know how Srijan-da had found out.

'It's not important how I got your number, Mallar. Tell me what you're doing over the weekend. Come over on Saturday, Srijan-da will make Chettinad chicken for you.'

Saturday arrived. I'd spent each of the four intervening nights imagining the weight of his body on me, drawing his warmth like a sheet over myself. I couldn't remember everything any more—what exactly was the man like? But what I remembered was enough to weave the sheet and cover myself with it.

Srijan-da had rented a place near T-Nagar in Chennai. A lovely, elegant neighbourhood. Many of the houses had their staircases outside the building. The steps led to a veranda, shared by the two flats on the same floor. His was the second one. I followed Srijan-da. As we negotiated the stairs, my anxiety kept rising, one step at a time. I was quite embarrassed, I wasn't sure why. Fortunately, he was ahead of me and couldn't see my expression.

When we went in, my embarrassment dissolved. Seated inside was a young man of South Indian appearance.

'Hi, I'm Ranganath, call me Ranga.'

'This is Mallar, Ranga. A childhood friend of my cousin's. This is my flatmate Ranganath. His full name is a tough one to pronounce, even I don't know it very well.'

Srijan-da introduced us in English.

Ranganath wasn't much of a talker, he sat on the mattress with his nose buried in his laptop. Just as well. He was doing his work quietly—and I was doing mine, which was to gaze at Srijan-da as he sliced onions, ginger and garlic. A tennis match was under-way on the TV, the sound muted, with Srijan-da providing the commentary, which sounded almost like a soliloquy, because Ranganath's eyes, ears and even nose were directed at his laptop, while my eyes were on Srijan-da, and I had no idea about my ears since I knew nothing of tennis.

Noticing that I was in a trance, Srijan-da said, 'Come into the kitchen, help Srijan-da.'

I jumped to my feet at once, but his flatmate was having none of it.

'No way, you're our guest, relax, we'll handle it.' Ranganath had made out what Srijan-da had said in Bangla because two of the words, *kitchen* and *help*, were in English.

After all these years, it seemed to me that Srijan-da was finally a human being. Earlier I used to think of him as the prince of my dreams, or a fairy-tale hero. Now both of us had changed, and so had my way of seeing. Besides, when someone's slicing onion and garlic in front of you, they seem much more human.

It was Ranganath who cooked the Chettinad chicken, Srijan-da was the helper. Now I knew why one Bengali had invited another one for a heavily South Indian meal. Ranganath had told Srijan-da to wash the banana leaves carefully, drain the water off them, lay them on the table, and serve three kinds of sides. The first was cucumber raita; the second, moistened moong dal with raw carrots; and the third, a sweet pickle.

'Since you're visiting our land, Mallar, we'll feed you exactly the way we eat here.'

'Mallar is like family, Ranga,' said Srijan-da. 'He's like a little brother to me. No need for formalities.'

Apparently, I was like a little brother to him.

Coarse red rice and Chettinad chicken. In South India, the banana leaf does the job of boosting the aroma of the food the way sal-leaf plates do back home. Srijan-da was grinning, I knew why.

'There's something very interesting this boy does, you know, Ranga. He sniffs the food before eating it.'

Something really surprised me. From laying out the banana leaves and thinly slicing the cucumber for the raita to arranging everything in a particular way, Ranga was something of a perfectionist. Since Srijan-da was nothing of the sort, I was equally surprised that he and Srijan-da could co-habit as flatmates. He used to scold us for small lapses while gardening, but that wasn't so much in pursuit of perfection as it was to throw his weight around with us younger boys. And now here he was, happily following someone else's orders. The man had certainly changed.

I thought of asking, *What magic web has Ranga spun around you?*, but then it occurred to me that our time was limited and it was pointless wasting it with interrogation. As the guest, my job was to concentrate on the food, so that was what I did.

'You know, Mallar, this Ranga is very finicky. Still I tolerate him and live under the same roof. Do you know why?' Srijan-da was speaking in English.

'Why?'

'You just ate what he's made and you're still asking that question?'

'Oh!'

'How can you leave someone who cooks so well?'

I wondered, *Would you have lived with me if I'd been as good a cook, Srijan-da?*

Obviously, I didn't ask the question.

'So Mallar, what are you in our city for?' Ranga asked.

'I'm here for some academic collaboration.'

Anyway, Srijan-da and I left in his car around two in the afternoon. 'Let me take you to Spencer Plaza, it used to be India's biggest shopping mall once.' This was for the benefit of his flatmate. Where Srijan-da took me was fifty kilometres away, to the town of Mahabalipuram, witness to fifteen hundred years of history.

After growing up and becoming financially independent, you couldn't quite elope with a beloved as you could have five years ago. What would you get away from? And from whom? I was quite thrilled that Srijan-da and I ran away after telling Ranganath a lie or two.

2

Mahabalipuram—or Mamallapuram as it was called—had a very old history. The temples here were between thirteen and fourteen hundred years old, the most famous among them being the Shore Temple. Few temples of this size in India were older that this. Although it was fifty metres from the sea, the roar of the waves made it seem as if it sat inside the Bay of Bengal. The temple looked like a giant stone chariot, moving forward, cutting through the tempestuous sea. The structure may have been of stone, but the scene appeared remarkably animated.

Ocean waves, rock temple. Despite this total contrast, they had been giving each other company for over a thousand years. For all their efforts, the waves had not been able to pull the rock temple into the depths of the indomitable sea. The rocks had stood there, deep in their penance. For each side knew how to live with its opposite, how to survive alongside its antithesis.

The ocean and the rock temple seemed to have signed a pact. An agreement to maintain a distance, to view each other's beauty from afar and go no further. Or else, like many other temples on seashores, this one too might have made its way to the bottom of the ocean, dancing in joy to the rhythm of the waves, and the sea god would have enriched his treasure trove with spoils from the temple's exquisite art.

'Isn't your flatmate going to ask where we've run away and why we aren't returning at night?'

'Don't you remember the condition we set, Mallar?'

'Got it.'

'Got what?'

'We won't be discussing third persons.'

Srijan-da and his conditions! I'd met an even more difficult condition already—not so much a condition as it was a vow like the one Bhishma had taken in the Mahabharata. Bhishma's was not to marry, mine was not to love. The first thing I did every morning was to remind myself of the vow, only after which did I face Srijan-da, who reminded me of it yet again. This new condition that I had to meet for two days was nothing in comparison. Besides, I wasn't an adolescent any more.

Then it occurred to me that everything in life was conditional. Employment set conditions, as did marriage. Love alone wasn't enough for a marriage, many promises had to be made. Love had no limits, but marriage did. Believers said God had no beginning or end, that God was limitless, but for everyday rituals even God had to be confined to a frame. Real life was impossible unless the infinite was confined within limits. So I had no complaints about conditions.

The sea here was so choppy that a warning had been put up not to swim in it, below which was a tally of the number of people who had drowned each year. People still ventured into the waters. You couldn't live by heeding every warning sign.

After this we went off to see the Pancharatha Temple. Five temples in the form of chariots, with an elephant on sentry duty in front—all made of stone.

'See, these temples have no interiors,' Srijan-da pointed out. 'Solid rock, all the carvings are on the outer side.'

He was right, the temples had no interiors, let alone a sanctum. In other words, large rocks had been carved to form these structures wherever they stood on the ground, with reliefs being etched on the outer walls. The rest was solid stone, with only an occasional corridor here or there.

'When the beauty on the outside wall fills your heart, who needs to hammer away inside?' I knew from my experience it was useful to be satisfied with outer beauty, with appearance. You could keep yourself happy this way, and everyone else. No need to stir the pot lying within.

Srijan-da smiled. 'You've got quite a way with words.'

Along with other gods and goddesses, the figure of the androgynous Ardhnarishvara was carved on one of the temple walls. The left foot and ankle had ornaments, but there was none on the right. A raised breast on the left, a flat chest on the right. Curvaceous lines for the hips and arm on the left, straight wooden ones on the right. Several bangles on the left wrist, just two on the right. Different kinds of earrings on each ear. Wondrous imagination, marvellous cohabitation.

The next stop was the Mahishasuramardini Mandapa, a rock-cut cave. Such drama even in stone—while the goddess Durga and the demon Mahishashura fight, the fear and anxiety of the soldiers caught between them is palpable. And then the series of ambiguous sculpted images. Arjun or Bhagirath performs penance standing on one foot. Birds and beasts, sages and hermits everywhere. And a cat imitating the act of austerity. The scenes were laid out so as to suggest both Arjun's austerity and Ganga descending to earth. One work of art with two stories, existing together, one concealed by the other—both true, both false, both visible, both hidden—but each a full-fledged story in its own right.

Leaving the thousand-year-old habitation behind, we went on to the more modern city of Pondicherry, an hour or two away by road. A former French colony, it had retained its French characteristics in some ways. Many of the buildings were French in style. A piece of France in India. The place where we were staying the night was not so much a hotel as it was a homestay or bed-and-breakfast. The building was about a hundred years old. There were rafters beneath the ceiling, and a courtyard in the middle of the two-storeyed house. The rooms had French windows with railings outside, balcony-less balconies. The wooden furniture, several bronze busts and oil-lamps were, however, Tamil in style. It was a confluence of French and Tamil cultures.

I was lying on the bed and quite literally counting the beams on the ceiling, as the Bengali saying goes, for the lack of anything better to do, when the phone rang. It was Srijan-da's mobile, he was in the bathroom. I looked at the name. Shilpi. I was about to take the phone to Srijan-da when I heard him say, 'I'm done, I'll come out and take the call.'

'Yes, hi Shilpi . . . just got here. No no, not with Ranganath . . . nor Rishabh or Samir . . . you don't know him . . . not exactly a friend, Mallar is my cousin's classmate . . . a boy, really . . . a really good boy, doesn't drink or smoke or do drugs . . . if I wanted to drink, I'd have come with them . . . don't worry . . . bye.'

Cousin's classmate! A boy, really!

Emerging from the bathroom wrapped in a towel, Srijan-da said as he put on his T-shirt, 'What are you staring at me for, you naughty boy! Didn't you hear what I told Shilpi: Mallar is such a good boy, quiet and restrained. And here you are . . .'

I wasn't staring at him at all. I did have some shame, after all. The cupboards here had full-length mirrors, I was stealing a look at his reflection, but his eyes were sharp enough to catch me out.

'So who's Shilpi?'

Srijan-da gave me a sharp, significant look.

'All right, I remember the condition, you don't have to remind me,' I said.

'Tell me what it was anyway, or you'll forget.'

'Are you a schoolteacher?'

Srijan-da got dressed and said, 'So Mr Conditions Apply, can we make our dinner plans now? Or does that also belong to the future according to the conditions you've set?'

'Of course not, we can definitely discuss today's plans. Come on, I'll treat you to French food.'

'All right!'

'Nice name you've got for me. Mr Conditions Apply.'

Many came to Pondicherry from Chennai for the weekend. We were looking for a French restaurant when we ran into a group of Srijan-da's former colleagues outside a pub.

'This is Mallar. My cousin's friend.'

It looked like this was my only identity—even though Srijan-da knew very well I had ended that particular friendship seven years ago. They introduced themselves one by one. One of the women, smartly dressed in a floral shirt and matching nail polish, said, 'Hi, I'm Ruhi. Why don't you join us, it'll be fun.' They kept coaxing Srijan-da, but he turned them down, telling them we were looking specifically for French food.

'He's always got a readymade excuse to avoid us,' Ruhi told me accusingly. Then she added, 'And Srijan, that suspicious gentleman, what's his name, does he still live with you? I forget his name.'

'Ranganath.'

I couldn't tell why a completely harmless person like Ranganath was the object of Ruhi's suspicion.

As we climbed up the stairs of the French restaurant, Srijan-da told me, 'I always have to prepare a reason to avoid Ruhi.'

'The poor thing has a crush on you.'

'You bet,' said Srijan-da, adjusting his hair.

'Shall we have spaghetti, Srijan-da?'

'Of course, but you can't have French food without crepes.'

I discovered crepes were a lot like dosa, though they were made with flour and the filling was meat.

'What's all this, are you actually eating without sniffing the dish first?'

'What can I do, I'm hungry.'

Srijan-da began even before I could ask, 'Are you wondering why people don't like Ranganath?'

'Why don't they?'

'He's actually a genius.'

'I see.'

'These people are his colleagues. I used to work in the same company once, which was when I met Ranganath. He's been planning his own start-up for the past six months. Ranganath's former flatmate used to keep his eyes and ears open, so all kinds of rumours about the start-up plans began to swirl in their office. So Ranganath began looking for a new flatmate.'

'Oh.'

'One morning I woke up rubbing my eyes to find him ringing my doorbell with all his luggage. He'd heard somewhere that my flatmate had moved to another town. He's taken shelter with me ever since.'

'OK.'

'And look, Srijan-da doesn't have the habit of eavesdropping. I can keep things to myself. So his secret is my secret.'

I said to myself, *You're a storehouse of secrets, you harbour so many of them.* What I uttered aloud was, 'Yes, but you just spilt this one.' What I didn't say was, *You also broke the promise about not talking of other people.* Perhaps the red wine he was sipping had made him forget it.

'I can trust you with any secret.'

With a sigh I reflected, *Sure you can, we're furtive people, everything we do remains in our deepest dreams, we never let our secrets out.*

'A Bengali and a Tamil, don't you have problems?'

'Why should I? Some distance because of language is a good thing.'

Indeed. Distance is good, it's useful.

Dessert was crepes too, but sweet ones. A lot like the patishapta we ate back home, except it had a filling of peanut butter. It was midnight by the time we finished eating. On the way back, we stood at the edge of the rocky beach and watched the darkness of the sea for some time. The roar of the waves in the dark seemed more mysterious. Their restlessness, smothered by the black night, provoked more contemplation.

'Let's go, baby, it's late. And these mosquitoes!'

'Five minutes?'

'Oh God. Don't they bite you?'

'I'm used to it. In the darkness of your outhouse, they . . .'

Srijan-da suddenly stopped fidgeting, calmed down, and looked at me a little indifferently.

'Never mind all that,' I said, 'let's go back.'

In the seclusion of the night, the French-style bungalows looked charming. I was dribbling a pebble with my foot when Srijan-da said, 'See that guy there? Kick the pebble at his shins.'

'Honestly! Do you want me to get beaten up?'

He stole the pebble with his foot.

'Should I?'

'What are you doing? What a strange man you are.'

'You're strange too. You really thought I'd kick it at him? Do you believe everything? You have peculiar fears.'

He wasn't wrong. I am a little too credulous. Thank goodness the buildings had no eyes or ears—you could do these crazy things in their presence, things you couldn't do in daylight in front of people. I showed Srijan-da a clump of flowers that had bloomed at night in front of one of the houses. Yellow and white, they had lit up the garden under the shade of the leaves. 'Night-flowering jasmine. So many flowers bloom only at night.'

We kicked the pebble all the way to the hotel.

Back in our room, I was taking off my sweat-soaked shirt when Srijan-da said, 'You used to be chubby five years ago. Have you been working on losing weight?'

'Dropped fifteen kilos.'

'Doesn't feel that way, baby. Maybe five.'

'Really? I have actually lost fifteen.'

'Is that so? Doesn't look like it. Let me check.'

'How will you check.'

'I'll show you.'

'What're you doing, not now, what're you doing, let go!'

It all happened without warning. Not everything was in my hands, much of it was in his. Even I was. My body was in his arms and his hips were between my legs.

'You never lifted me up like this when I was a kid.'

'You hardly visited. Even when you did, you wouldn't come near me. You always escaped, didn't you?'

Whether it was passion or my simply weight, those arms of his were trembling. Finally, I had managed to look into his eyes. I didn't answer his question but only told myself, *Of course I escaped, you're such a villain.*

3

Srijan-da practically threw me on the bed from his arms. Then he gave me a long, piercing look. *What do you want?* his eyes were saying. He uttered it too, 'What do you want?' Srijan-da knew quite well what I wanted, and what he himself wanted. I knew him, he liked asking this question, he liked reading the anxiety in my eyes that did not answer his question. He liked hearing from me what I wanted, seeing in my eyes what I wanted. The divine forester was all-knowing, but he took pleasure in hearing his disciple pray, in seeing the plea in the disciple's eyes. But I wasn't a teenager any more. So I intentionally delayed my response, trying to provoke a shade of impatience in his gaze. This was no longer the game from my childhood, it was a different one.

My eyes were red, I couldn't see clearly but still I wanted to. There were many scenes that simply have to be seen. I hadn't slept well at night to begin with, and then I'd set the alarm for five in the morning to watch the sunrise from the rock beach. There was no sand here, only large rocks, on one of which we sat down. Srijan-da wasn't particularly interested in the sunrise, he fell asleep with his head in my lap. It wasn't a big deal in South India for a man to sleep with his head in another man's lap. A familiar sight, in fact. No one cared.

Anyway, the sun began to peep out from the sea. The dark water became a shade of grey, which slowly turned to gold. I tried to awaken the man lying in my lap.

'Don't bug me, you brat, let me sleep. You troubled me all night. I've seen plenty of sunrises.' He buried his face deeper in my belly.

'Your stubble is pricking me.'

'Through your shirt?'

'Yes.'

'Let it.'

Then he said, 'Baby, what'll you do if your husband tries to bury his stubbled face in your belly?'

So Srijan-da slept with his head in my lap, and I saw the sunrise alone, and along with it the tender golden sunlight falling on his face. I was shielding his face from the sun—not because he'd scold me if he woke up, but because I hadn't seen the tranquil beauty of his face, like the water of a lake, when last night we groped each other's bodies as if playing blind man's buff. Now I gazed at the stillness of his serene, satiated face, such a contrast to the roaring waves in the half-light-half-darkness of dawn. I'd never see it again once his eyes opened because of the sun.

I said to myself, *I wanted to find out about Shilpi last night, but I didn't ask. Just as well you set the conditions. Thank heavens no third person is allowed into our world. Or the night would have belonged to someone else instead of you and me. The night is brief, and by daylight you're someone else—so why waste time on questions and answers? You're asleep in my lap, the morning is unfolding before me, and yet it is last night that appears in front of my eyes. What was it that you said—so many flowers bloom only at night. Let your eyes remain shut, and let me remain here protecting you with my shadow, for if I don't, this gentle sunshine will soon turn harsh and open your eyes, snapping this magical web of illusion.*

The web snapped soon enough with a call on Srijan-da's mobile. From a hint of the voice, I gathered it was yesterday's caller. Shilpi. Srijan-da set all the conditions, but if it was up to me, I'd have definitely set one condition for him—to switch off his mobile for two days.

I played with the waves while he was busy talking on the phone. Not the waves in the sea but the waves in his hair. What did I care who was calling him? We were each doing our own work—his was to talk on the phone, and mine, to play with his curls. His was to smile gently with the phone clamped to his ear, mine was to savour the innocence of his face, like that of a suddenly awakened child. His was to listen quietly on the phone, mine was to wait. When I stopped playing, he looked at me quizzically with the mobile still at his ear, a look that said, *Why'd you stop, it was nice, go on with what you were doing.*

4

'Get up, boy.'

Srijan-da sat still for some time even after finishing his phone conversation. For I was dozing with my head resting on his back.

In a sleep-laced voice I said, 'First tell me what people chatter so much about on the phone. How do they have so many things to say?'

'Seems to me you need a dunking in the sea to wake up.'

'Tell me please, do lovers have so much to tell each other?' I wonder if I'd have asked these questions if I hadn't been half asleep.

'Who says? To whom? What lovers are you talking about?'

'That's for you to know. Even in love I never learnt to talk so much. I only filled my sketchbook to tell the story of my love.'

'Let's go back to the hotel, baby—time for breakfast.'

I understood my words could be dangerous. I had no control over what I was saying in my half-asleep state. Ending the conversation, we walked from the beach to the street.

Over the past five years, I had certainly tried to stay away from Srijan-da, but I hadn't forgotten him. I liked living in an imaginary world. I had spent ever so many nights conjuring up the scenes—we had met again somewhere, we were tending to a garden, I was dressing him up as a groom again. I was sure we'd meet again someday. When we did, I'd tell him all kinds of things, and in turn he'd do all kinds of mischief with me. If we sat down to talk, perhaps an entire night would pass. I used to wonder— when we met, would I say *I've thought about you often*, or would I pretend I had great willpower and was not like the lovelorn heroines of yore? There was no counting the number of such conversations I had imagined. What I hadn't imagined was that when we met, we would make a pact to measure our words.

Breakfast was idlis and a tri-coloured hot-and-sour chutney. A South Indian filter coffee dispelled my sleepiness, and together we headed for the market. Shilpi had asked for some junk jewellery Pondicherry was famous for. We bought some, all made with strange, large stones. I got some for myself too. Also a few inexpensive necklaces made with cowries, seashells and oyster shells. Srijan-da wanted to know what I was going to do with these— would I wear them myself? I told him what I meant to do with them, lay in the future, and therefore it was not to be discussed according to the agreed terms and conditions. At this, he shot me a sideways glance. I did have a plan for these necklaces in the near future though.

We walked through the crowded market after our shopping was done. I was in front, Srijan-da followed me with his phone clamped to his ear, clutching the strap of my sling bag to guide himself. We'd be in trouble if we got separated in the crowd, so this was the best solution. We ran into Ruhi as well. Srijan-da's hands were occupied with the mobile and my sling bag, his tongue was busy talking to Shilpi. Ruhi flashed a smile and winked lightly at the busy man. And the gentleman in question got quite flustered trying to manage the call with Shilpi, the bag slung from my shoulder and Ruhi's wink all at the same time.

If someone on the street greeted you, you were supposed to greet them back, you were supposed to return their hi or hello with a hi or a hello. Not doing this was rude. I didn't know how to respond to a wink. But Srijan-da didn't have to fret about this, because instead of interrupting his call, Ruhi vanished in the crowd.

Srijan-da looked over his shoulder, still holding the phone, and so did I. Ruhi had melded into the throng of people.

Srijan-da was so busy on his phone that, irritated, I freed myself and went off to look at the shops selling cheap but fancy things. Catching up from behind, he said, 'You think you can just run away? What if you're lost in the crowd?'

'Don't worry, I won't be lost. I can't blend into the crowd very well, as you know.'

After checking out of the hotel, our next destination was Paradise Island Beach. We left in the car.

'Srijan-da will now show you something truly first class, Mallar.'

'Hadn't you left the third person out of our grammar?'

'I had indeed.'

'But you refer to yourself in the third person most of the time—Srijan-da will take you to blah blah, Srijan-da said blah blah, Srijan-da will cook blah blah.'

'Is that so?'

'It's called illeism.'

'Ille . . . what?'

'Illeism. Referring to oneself not as I but in the third person. Many European and American leaders speak this way.'

'Oh really! You seem to be supremely knowledgeable about this.'

You could only drive up to a point, after which you had to take a speedboat. Riding in one for the first time, I felt quite frightened, but it also gave me a chance to hold on to Srijan-da. It was impossible imagine that such a desolate island and beach existed so close to the city. Perhaps because we had arrived a short while after lunch, there was only a handful of people besides us. Everyone kept to themselves.

There were two things I liked doing on a beach, and both needed another person. The first was to walk hand in hand along the line where sand met the water, with the waves occasionally playing over our feet. We walked this way for some time. Looking over my shoulder, I saw four sets of footprints stretching back some way, after which the sea had wiped them out. Let the sea do that, I had no regrets, I was pleased at having left the prints of two pairs of feet between the two of us, even if for a few moments.

And then the second thing.

'Take off your shirt,' I told Srijan-da.

'Behave yourself, what is it you want here? No shame?'

'Everyone takes their shirt off at the beach.'

'I didn't put on sunscreen.'

'A little sun won't turn your light skin brown in a minute.'

'Can't say no to you, can I?'

I took some wet sand from the shoreline. It had turned dark with moisture. Slowly, I smeared it on Srijan-da's body.

'You should have been an idol maker, Mallar.'

'No, I'm happy with my debonair god Kartik.'

'With all this sand, you've turned me into a different god— Lord Shiva covered in ash.'

It was amusing to see the caramel physique turn dark.

'You're getting a free body scrub.'

Then I put the necklace of chunky seashells on his chest. Its brilliant whiteness looked impossibly beautiful against his black-sand-smeared torso. I added another item, a necklace of stones, and wound chains of smaller cowries and shells several times around his wrists.

'So this was what baby had in mind? This is why all those necklaces and chains.'

I wound similar chains around his ankles too.

'Who are you dressing me up as?'

'Assume you're Varuna, the sea god, imagine this is how he dresses to be worshipped. Conventional divine attire won't do.'

Five years ago too, I used to love dressing Srijan-da up. I'd even dressed him as a groom. But this was altogether different.

Now I knocked his sitting figure flat on the ground. He wasn't prepared for the shove, but he dealt with it. Then I began to massage his chest and stomach lightly with my feet.

'Should you be disrespecting someone older than you by touching him with your foot?'

'I should.'

Five years ago, Srijan-da wasn't so obedient. Five years ago too, I had dressed him up with flowers and leaves and colours, but I had to coax and cajole him for this. Now I was astonished to see he had handed the reins to me. People did change with time.

He had restrained himself all this while, but now I could hear a series of pleasurable *aah*-s and *oh*-s emanating from his lips. I told him to turn over, and massaged his back with my feet. He was breathing so fast now that it was blowing away the sand beneath his face. I don't remember using the speed of sand to measure anyone's breath before. The sea was deafening, which I was happy about. I didn't want anyone else to hear the sound of Srijan-da's voice or his breathing. Let them merge into the roar of the waves. The sun was as strong as ever, it made the sand on Srijan-da's back glisten.

He turned over with his back on the sand to face me, his body swelling and shrinking as he inhaled and exhaled. I could hear a soft whooping sound nearby. Srijan-da turned towards it and then pointed it out to me. I saw it too—a seagull, playing in the water, fluttering its wings. Birds were perpetually restless. I didn't know who among the three of us was most impatient right then. Drawing my attention to this new scene, Srijan-da suddenly pulled me by my arm so that I sank into muddy sand, or rather, into the man whose skin had been muddied black by the sand.

'Don't get me dirty, I'm warning you, let go.'

Who was listening? The more I tried to free myself, the tighter the clay figure held me to itself.

'What about the fact that you got me all muddy? It's wrong only if I do it?'

'Yes.'

He had an iron grip on my wrist, which he was twisting.

'Let's go to the car,' he said.

Brushing the sand off his body with his singlet, he put on his clothes. We took the speedboat back to the car park. I wasn't frightened this time, but Srijan-da was holding my arm firmly and had locked his eyes with mine, as though I was about to escape. It felt like we were measuring the hunger in each other's eyes in that heaving speedboat. From the car park, we drove towards a deserted spot. Sunshades, secured with suction pads, darkened the car windows. He reclined the front seats.

I'd always been a little claustrophobic. Many people have fantasies of doing it inside a car, but I was choking, I didn't feel comfortable at all. I tried to give Srijan-da as much pleasure as I could. After a while, he caught on.

'I won't force you, baby. Let's stop here if you aren't comfortable.'

'I'm trying.'

'Baby, I'm happy with what I've got from you, with as much as I've got from you. All right? Keep the rest for some time in the future.'

But we weren't supposed to bring up the future.

5

Over and over again, I have lost this game too
My hours slip by, matching tunes with you.

Srijan-da scolded me mildly for dozing in the seat beside his, at which I asked him to play a song. It was this song of Tagore's that began to play.

I didn't know about winning or losing, but there was no choice but to match my tune to his. Trouble was when the tune you were trying to match snapped abruptly. The condition Srijan-da had set was certainly strange, but his idea of creating an imaginary world during these two days, with space for just the two of us and only one tense of time, wasn't a bad one. An immobile rock in the path of the irresistible torrent of time, which would not drift away in its current, which both of us could clutch onto. But there was a flaw in the condition. Talking of anyone else was forbidden, but their phone calls were not. So Srijan-da's phone rang and the melody snapped.

'Take the call,' said Srijan-da, driving.

I did. It was Shilpi. 'Finally getting to speak to you. Is your Dadabhai taking you around lots of places? He spins people off their feet.'

Now she had also turned him into my brother. Can two men of unequal age not be friends or something else?

'Yes, I'm enjoying myself.'

'The junk jewellery is nice. He sent pictures. Said you chose them.'

'Not really, we bought them together.'

'Yes, I know him. And you had French wine yesterday, Chardonnay. My favourite wine.'

'Yes, so good.'

'He didn't drink and drive, did he?'

'No, we walked back.'

'You have to watch out for these things, he's in your hands now.'

'Please don't worry, madam . . .'

'Am I your grandmother?'

'What?'

'What's all this madam business?'

Srijan-da exclaimed, 'You're asking questions like a grand-mother. OK, we're about to stop for lunch.'

'Don't get sunstroke wandering about in the sun like last time,' said Shilpi.

If only Shilpi could see how I've given him sunburn, I thought.

'No, we aren't going out in the sun at all—tell her, Mallar, are we going out in the sun?'

For some reason, it felt as though Srijan-da wasn't particu-larly disinclined to hand over the reins to someone else, to follow instructions. The fact was that once you submitted yourself to someone else, you could do whatever you liked, because then it was the other person's responsibility—you didn't have to answer to yourself. Who knew whether this was the reason for the change in him?

Before ending the call, Shilpi said, 'Srijan is a wonderful person, Mallar, he keeps everyone happy. Me, his family, his flatmate, everyone. He must be ensuring you're happy too. And for this he can lie quite easily. Like he did just now.'

We were sick of Continental and South Indian food, so we decided to eat a Chinese meal. The restaurant was situated between the backwaters and the sea. It had a thatched roof and was open on all sides. The view was beautiful all around. Who'd have known the same waters could be both calm and wild? Srijanda said while entering the restaurant, 'I'm still itching from all the sand you put on me.'

'Come, we'll dunk you in the sea there and clean it off.'

'Shut up, you wretch, nothing but devilish ideas in that head of yours.'

We ordered noodles and chilli fish.

'You've been paying for all the meals, I'll pay today.'

'Stop. Put that wallet back in your pocket—right now.'

'Then let's go Dutch.'

'Listen to the Bengali talking about going Dutch. Are you putting that wallet back or not?'

Glumly, I returned my wallet to my pocket.

'Baby, you're just like my little brother. How can I not take you around and pay for you during these two days?'

'Like your brother? I'm like your brother!'

'Oh not in that sense. Relax Mallar, don't be angry.'

'I *am* relaxed.'

'Chill. Calm down, baby.'

Far from calming down, with nothing else at hand, I threw my napkin at his face. He wisely tucked it into the back of his chair.

'You're not getting it back.'

He knew I'd throw it at him again if I did.

'And why are you looking at the cutlery?' he asked.

'Relax—I'm not that violent.'

'You never know, I haven't seen even this kind of violence before. How quiet you used to be.'

I was indeed. Why was I feeling so unsettled? Before speaking to Shilpi on the phone, I used to think of her as a voice. In the background. After talking to her, she felt like a person, a living being, someone who existed, who had a personality, wants and needs, claims too. Whether she was in front of my eyes or not, she was real.

I didn't know who Shilpi was. Was she Srijan-da's lover? Fiancée? Wife? An arranged match? Or was she a playtime companion like me? Or perhaps merely a friend, a very nice, caring friend who kept track of little things? For some reason, I felt she wouldn't vanish in a crowd.

This wasn't new to me. So many people had entered and left my own playroom. I didn't even remember each of them, I didn't even ask everyone for their name. They too had other people in their lives, they weren't a bunch of flowers without roots and branches. Then why was I wracking my brains over Srijan-da and Shilpi?

Maybe I could be kept happy with food and travel. What was it that Shilpi had said—*Srijan-da can keep everyone happy.* But to keep Shilpi happy, it needed extra effort—stories had to be made up. I wondered why stories didn't have to be made up to keep me happy.

With these thoughts running through my head, I sat down on the bench beneath the sacred fig tree and began to doze. The backwaters ran next to the restaurant and this tree stood beside it. Sacred figs had always given me shelter. Its shade and the gentle breeze blowing over the backwaters all but put me to sleep. In the distance, I could see Srijan-da on the steps leading down to the water, his phone clamped to his ear. He was signalling to me to go sit next to him. But at that moment, I was drawn more by the cool comfort of the tree than the warmth of a human body. Lying down on my side on the bench and drawing my knees up to my chest, I fell asleep without even realizing it.

6

I woke up abruptly.

'Come on, baby, don't you have school? Don't you have to pack your bag?'

'No-o-o, don't tickle!'

'The teacher will scold me if you're late. Good children go to bed early and rise early. Get up, get up. Have to get baby ready for school.'

'Don't tickle me any more, please.'

There were days when you went to sleep sad and woke up laughing. And as you laughed, it occurred to you no one was likely to wake you up this way on other days. If only someone would!

'The way you were sleeping beneath the tree, I thought you'd wake up any moment, put on your uniform and go to school.'

When he saw me sitting on the bench even after this, with sleepy eyes and a smiling face, seemingly detached from everything, Srijan-da said, 'I have to go to work tomorrow, don't I? Come on, get into the car.'

The East Coast Road was lovely. It ran from Pondicherry to Chennai via Mahabalipuram. Plenty of green, with the Bay of

Bengal alternately surrendering itself to us and withdrawing into the distance. I liked the occasional invitation from the sea. Far better than the tedium of sitting by it all day was its sporadic appearance, beckoning to you each time.

With the window rolled down, I tasted the salty breeze of the Coromandel Coast fluttering into the car.

'You look like you're having a conversation with the sea.'

Of course I was. The sea was telling me, *Instead of making sketches to be carefully framed, sometimes it's better to just draw on the sand. You won't have to worry about wiping it away. There are many drawings where you cannot remove every stroke with an eraser but a drawing on sand is wiped off automatically by the sea.*

'Hey, Mallar, are you mad at me?'

'Of course not.'

'You were sketching yesterday—show me.'

The first one I showed him was of the Shore Temple in Mahabalipuram.

'How beautifully you've captured the architectural details.'

Next, the statue of Gandhi in Pondicherry.

'I still have the sketch you gave me.'

'Does the man still sleep the same way beneath trees?'

'He does. And the boy still keeps watch. So that the man can't run away.'

'They've grown much older now though.'

'Show me the next page. There seems to be one more sketch.'

'Haven't completed it. I'll show you some other time.'

'Please show me now.'

I did. Srijan-da said, 'There you are, the man's still sleeping. But this time on the boy's lap.'

'Perhaps the boy's no longer afraid the man will run away.'

'I know. But why is the sun rising on the southern side of the rock beach?'

'Not showing you anything any more.'

'Send it to me when you complete it. With your signature and date. You will, right?'

A little later Srijan-da continued, 'There's a poem on the page after that, show me.'

'No way, it's a lousy poem.'

'So what, read it out.'

'No, you read it.'

'All right.' Balancing the sketchbook on the steering wheel Srijan-da began reading, *'The flower that only . . .'*

'Is that any way to read poetry? Read with some heart.'

'The flower that blooms at night alone,
That fears daylight,
The grass that only sways in the breeze,
That has no desire to spread its wings
And fly.
The silent pursuer tries
To make it bloom, make it float,
In vain is his pursuit.'

It was quite late by the time we got back to Chennai. I had fallen asleep in the car and had had a strange dream—of drawing in the sand and having everything wiped off, of a wild wind and cascades of seawater erasing it all. Srijan-da nudged me awake. The dream kept floating in my head and I mused, *Not everything needs to leave behind a mark, not everything even should—there are many things not meant to be held on to.*

'Stay the night at my place. I'll drop you to the university early tomorrow.'

'No, I have a deadline, I have to work when I get back.'

'All right, I'll drop you at the university right now. But you won't get dinner at this hour. There's a late-night eatery around here, I'll treat you to Malabar parotta and korma.'

On the way to the university after a dinner of Malabar parotta, korma, and cucumber-onion salad, he asked, 'Your Srijan-da is a terrible guy, isn't he?'

'Why do you say that?'

'Sets conditions every time.'

Just as well he does, I thought. *Without those conditions, I'd have been madly in love with him by now. Those conditions have kept me from love, stopped me from going mad.*

About to drive into the campus, Srijan-da stopped the car in an unlit spot and said, 'What is it, baby, is my breath smelling of onions?'

'No.'

'Well, then?'

'What do you mean?'

'Come closer.'

Thoughts of Shilpi were still swirling in my head. Pushing them away for a moment, I held out my lips. I knew when he called me Mallar and when he addressed me as baby.

Srijan-da was right, some flowers did bloom at night. You shouldn't disturb them when they slept during the day, shouldn't cajole them to blossom. Their comfort was in the darkness.

Srijan-da seemed to measure the length of my upper and lower lips with his fingers before holding out his own. When people kissed at the beginning of lovemaking, there was anxiety and disquiet, for it was only the prelude. But when the kiss was the only thing, when the kiss was the climax, when people knew there would be nothing after the kiss, then all the emotion, all the sensations, all hidden aches were combined in it. For there was nothing afterwards.

'Let me drive you to the guesthouse.'

It was about a mile from the university gate.

In front of the guesthouse, he said, 'Now what?'

'Meaning?'

'You're going back next Sunday, right? Come over on Saturday if you're free.'

'I'll think about it.'

'Think about it now.'

'Do you remember the condition we agreed to, Srijan-da?'

'Got it.'

'Repeat it anyway.'

'We won't talk of the past or the future.'

'So let's keep Saturday for Saturday. Now let me go.'

I climbed up the stairs of the guesthouse. Stopping where I wouldn't be seen, I looked at Srijan-da as he gazed at the empty staircase for a minute or so. The stairs and Srijan-da seemed to be measuring how long each would wait. Then Srijan-da went back to his car and started the engine. The headlights disappeared in no time amid the impenetrable darkness of the trees.

BOOK THREE

Looking Back

You answered in monosyllables,
Some, you didn't even respond to.
Conveyed with an impatient wave—
Why talk of all this,
Silence is so much better.

1

On one side, Hercules battling with the sea monster. On the other, a burly soldier covered in wounds gets to his feet to fight afresh—there's agony on his face, anxiety in his eyes, but his body radiates extraordinary confidence. Two thousand years separated them. Nude figures of powerfully built men stood everywhere. I was in the Louvre, Paris.

The Louvre was a thousand-page manuscript documenting millennia of Western art. Artists had carved these figures out of marble hundreds, even thousands of years ago. With great labour, they had infused these bodies of stone with emotions, fears, agonies and resolve, lovingly carving every single muscle, believing nudity to be a pure form of truth.

Gazing at such a statue, I told Srijan-da, 'If I'd been a sculptor, I'd have made you my model.'

'Indecent thoughts are all you have.'

I hadn't expected to come back with Srijan-da's story. Just because we lived in the same neighbourhood once upon a time didn't mean we'd run into each other constantly. So his return to my story wasn't natural. Even less so because I had tried my utmost to push him away. Whom was I to blame if he returned to my life nevertheless? And of all places to meet, Paris! But before telling the story of Paris, I must go back about six years.

About a month after I had returned from that trip to Chennai, my mother called to say, 'Guess what, your Srijan-da is getting married.'

In my mind, I laughed at *your Srijan-da*.

'How nice.'

'Engagement in December, wedding in March. The girl's name is Shilpi.'

Chikan called a couple of hours later.

'You'll come, right?'

I'd be crazy to, I told myself.

'I'll think about it, OK?'

'Will you come if Dadabhai asks you himself?'

I thought, *During that wedding ritual in which the couple showers puffed rice from a tray into the sacred fire, I'll throw the whole tray at your Dadabhai's face.*

'Listen Chikan, will it be right for people like me to attend the wedding of someone as honourable as your Dadabhai?'

'Please don't mind what I said as a kid. Come, we'd love to have you here.'

Which is all very well, I mused, *but do I care what you'd 'love to have'?*

'Will you come if Dadabhai asks you himself?' he asked again.

That Dadabhai also called. I said, 'I really can't, honestly. I know I said all those years ago I'd dress you up as a groom for your wedding with all my heart—but believe me, I don't have it in me any more.'

Eventually, I found myself back in our house in Birajpur after many years, on the occasion of Saraswati Puja. Every time I went home I inspected my bookshelves. Or, to be precise, the sketch-books I kept on them, and every time I debated whether to take them with me. Then, after some argument with myself, I'd decide that I'd take them only after I became strong-willed. It was better for them to remain on the strong bookshelves instead of being with a feeble-minded person. No need to disturb them. Let my childhood stay shelved, let me use a different sketchbook in my adult life.

I hadn't expected Srijan-da to be there at that time. The engagement had taken place and the wedding was not due for another three months—he wasn't supposed to be home in between. But then my mother told me the wedding had been can-celled soon after the engagement.

I was out on a walk near the railway station when I heard a motorbike and a familiar voice from behind.

'Oy rascal—and what are you doing here?'

We sat down on a bench for a cup of tea. Srijan-da looked beautiful sporting a thin beard and a red panjabi.

'We took the decision jointly. Shilpi is a wonderful girl, she used to love me very much, a love I wasn't capable of reciprocating.

She wanted us to share every moment of our lives. For instance, if I went anywhere she wanted updates all the time, and if she went anywhere she wanted me to listen patiently to all her descriptions of everyone and everything.'

'OK.'

'If I had a fever, I was supposed to text her my temperature every hour. I don't think I'd have survived so much love and caring.'

'OK.'

'Caring people are a little possessive too. I wouldn't have been able to offer even ten per cent of the time and affection she would lavish on me.'

I didn't know if these were really the reasons they'd called off the wedding, and neither was it necessary for him to justify it to me in such detail—I hadn't asked. I gave the same one-word reply: 'OK.'

'What do you mean OK?'

I sipped my tea.

'Come home.'

'I've got a fever coming on, I can't make it.'

I didn't have a fever or anything. Srijan-da put his hand on my forehead and then on both sides of my neck to gauge my temperature. I don't know what he discovered, but all he asked was, 'Are you taking medicines?'

Perhaps it would have been better if he hadn't touched me. Perhaps it would have been all right. My arteries and veins still felt a surge of electricity at that touch. Never mind, I'd learnt to resist. You're out shopping for expensive fish, and just because you have a few extra bucks in your pocket, you also pick up a cheap vegetable you fancy—great! But no self-respecting person wants to be that cheap vegetable. Neither did I.

Poor Srijan-da, he was single, maybe unhappy—but no matter how sympathetic this might make me feel, I wouldn't go there. I would truss up my arms, legs, nerves tightly and hold myself back, but I wouldn't go there. No matter how much my body responded to his touch, unless there was an invitation from his heart, I wouldn't go there.

2

Shiuli-di called.

'I saw three missed calls from you, Mallar. Sorry sweetie, I was in a meeting, is everything OK?'

'Would there be three missed calls if it was?'

'OK, what's happened?'

'I should have said yes to Srijan-da the other day. Was it right to say no?'

'Why shouldn't it be? You said no because you didn't care for his tone, for the way he spoke. You were absolutely right.'

'It isn't about whether my behaviour with him was right or wrong.'

'What's it about then?'

'About whether my behaviour with myself was right or wrong.'

'Can you tell me why this question has popped up after two years? I get it, it's that boyfriend of yours. Whenever you fight with Nikhil, these things occur to you. Right or wrong?'

'Nikhil isn't my boyfriend though. If he was, I'd have fought to my heart's content with him. I haven't quarrelled with him Oli-di.'

'OK then, tell me why you think you haven't been fair to yourself?'

'Maybe Srijan-da's tone wasn't a good one, but you know that's how he is, that's how he speaks. He's always pulling rank on me because I'm four years younger . . .'

' . . . And asks you to see him only if he feels the need. Love when he needs it, and when the need is met, a reminder of the no-love clause. Right?'

'No, it's just that . . .'

'Just that what?'

'Maybe calling off his marriage was an inflection point in his life. Maybe it was a new period of indecision and reflection. Maybe it would have helped him if I'd been with him, perhaps that was what he wanted.'

'If he wanted it, he'd have said it differently.'

'Who knows.'

'I'm saying it again, don't beat yourself up about what happened two years ago. You're fine, aren't you? With your day lover and your night lover, you're just fine.'

'The day lover isn't a lover, Oli-di. I really like cooking for him, he's just like a little brother.'

'And the night lover?'

'We never talk love, you know. He and I live in the land of eternal bliss. Talking is forbidden in this paradise. It disrupts our devotion to the god of lovemaking. This devotion needs undivided attention.'

'I get it, neither is a lover.'

'No, Oli-di.'

'So someone teaches you not to love and leaves, and you'll spend the rest of your life protecting yourself and not loving anyone.'

'That's how it'll be.'

'Sweetie, you and I will sit down one day and fix the definition of a lover. Whether it's the one you love cooking for, the one with whom you worship the god of lovemaking or the one you like recalling ten years later and weeping.'

'We'll do that.'

'You know, I used to have a lover with whom I used to love doing all three of these things.'

'What! But what happened to him?'

'What do you suppose? He's a husband now, not a lover any more.'

'I see what you mean.'

'See, all the poets from Jaidev to Chandidas have written a thousand poems about the incomplete love story of Radha and Krishna—at least one of them could have completed the story, could have written about their setting up a home together. No one did. Why not? Because no one would listen to a story like that, it would be a disaster. Have you heard of anyone who has written lyrics about the households of Satyabhama and Rukmini—the women who married Krishna?'

This did make me laugh. I said, 'Tell you what, I'm going to write about those two women sharing the same man. In the same lyric style.'

'So, the lover doesn't remain a lover very long. No use stressing about it.'

Shiuli-di, or Oli-di as I called her, was someone I'd turned into a sort of elder sister, with whom I could talk about these things and lighten my heart.

'I'll go now, Oli-di, it's almost time for the man of my nights.'

The bell rang.

'I think Harshit's here, Oli-di, I'll open the door.'

'Don't you want to love?' I'd once asked Harshit.

'Of course I do, there are so many things in the world I want to love,' he'd said. 'But where's the time?'

So another four years later came the unexpected meeting—a most dramatic one. And where do you suppose? In Paris! When I die and go to hell, I'll find Srijan-da there too.

I hadn't been in touch for years, deliberately. Some news used to trickle in through my parents, but even that dried up when they left the house in Birajpur and bought a flat in Kolkata to settle down there.

I was trying to get into a Paris Métro train. I was at the historic Hôtel de Ville station, named for a building. It wasn't a hotel though, but an administrative building—and the nerve centre of the French Revolution. So it was at this historic station that we met. There he was without warning, on the opposite platform. He saw me too. I was about to call out when the train arrived clattering on his platform, an eyesore popping up between the two of us. He had vanished by the time the train left. Had he got on the train? My train was entering too. Suddenly I felt a tug on my hood from the back. He was panting, he had run all the way.

'Mallar! Baby's in Paris now?'

'I'm here for a conference, some client visits too. What are you doing here?'

'I'm on job rotation. I'm here for about three months.'

I was still gazing at Srijan-da in surprise. He said, 'Paris is the fashion capital of the world. What on earth are you wearing?'

'I don't get fashion.'

'That's OK but get rid of the price tag at least.'

'Where is it?'

'Here,' he said and put his hand on my neck, inside my jacket. He was in a mischievous mood, I realized and refused to let him in. After this had gone on for a while, what he pulled out from the neck of my jacket was not the price tag but a small sticker the dry cleaner had attached for identification.

'And why are you getting goosebumps?'

If only I could have answered. Never mind.

I found some people around us staring in some surprise at our love play. Srijan-da gave them an awkward smile.

His place was far away, he was in a hurry. We decided to meet the next day, meaning Friday, at five in the evening outside the Louvre. The museum was open till nine on Fridays, we'd visit it together.

There was a doctor living inside my body whom I would often consult. Now the doctor asked if there was a threat of falling in love. *No*, I answered, *because I'm in the city for two weeks only. And these days I don't fall in love, I have romances. Do you have a romantic desire? All round the year. Onward, therefore.* I hugged Srijan-da before he was about to get on his train. The cold in Paris was excuse, reason and catalyst—all three—to do this. He didn't stop me. He's a little taller than me, I planted a light kiss between his chest and shoulders, as though I'd done it without knowing it. He seemed unprepared for this. 'The train's here,' he said, 'see you.'

I'd long nurtured the dream of visiting the Louvre. Now I was going there finally, and with Srijan-da, at that. The thought kept me awake all night. Clutching the pillow, I kept turning over from one side to the other. I parted the curtains to let the light in and make the room look magical, then drew them again because I couldn't sleep unless it was dark. Heroines of yore would get the hero's jacket, hold one sleeve out with her own, wrap the other sleeve around her shoulder and dance with it. I was crazy enough to use my own jacket. It was only right to dance when your heart was dancing. This was the jacket from which he'd tried to extricate the laundry tag. I laughed when I remembered this. I must have been at it till three in the morning.

They say Paris is the city of love. Let it be, I would have nothing to do with it. I reminded myself quickly of the old conditions.

3

Oedipus is confronted by the winged sphinx's question. It must have been a difficult one. The sphinx guards the city, her job is to ask a riddle. Only if she gets the right answer will she allow entry—she shoulders a crucial responsibility. Her face is unclear, her body is sunk in a mixture of light and shade. Oedipus' body is brightly lit. Unabashedly naked, he is the embodiment of Greek male beauty. His muscled body radiates both determination and composure. The sphinx is immersed in her question and hence only half-lit. Oedipus has the answer, which makes him confident and unrestrained. These were my thoughts as I viewed Francois Xavier Fabre's painting of Oedipus in Louvre. Although he used his intelligence to answer the riddle correctly and secure entry to the city, the luckless Oedipus could not eventually escape his fate. Let's keep that tale for another time.

Up next was Leonardo Da Vinci's *St John the Baptist*. A painting of a saint, but with a subtle sexual passion. Various portraits of Hercules—with the assertion of integrity in his nudity, a plea evident even in the flexing of his muscles. On one side is a painting of Hercules wrestling, and on the other he waits to create his own funeral pyre on his poisoned body. He is waiting for his lover Philoctetes, who is the only one with the right to light

Hercules' pyre. His body reveals his stark agony—from the poison, from the waiting.

The grace of the male body was the leitmotif of many of the paintings we saw at the Louvre. Not just in the expression in the eyes and the wrinkles on the faces, the emotions, the anxieties, the drama of the paintings were expressed in the creases on the muscles as well. The artists seemed to have spoken through the stiffness and the slackness, the firmness and the naturalness of the sinews.

Paris beyond the Louvre was just as colourful. The main gay district here was Le Marais. When we were done at the Louvre, I asked Srijan-da whether he was comfortable going to such a place.

'I'm in your hands—I can hardly say no, can I?' This was a favourite response was his, I'd heard it many times before.

I was surprised to see how comfortably and casually homosexual people were wandering around Le Marais, expressing their love or lust, as the case might be, for each other. I had seen many cities in the West, seen gay lives there, but I had seldom witnessed such comfort and casualness. Many of the businesses here were run by gay people. There were numerous restaurants and cafes and ice-cream parlours in Le Marais, many winding lanes too. We went to one of the restaurants for dinner.

The waitress was a garrulous woman. Preliminary greetings in this country were always in French, and then, if the customer was not very comfortable in the language, the waitstaff would try to use English. In her French-accented English, she asked whether we were friends.

'He's more than a friend.' I liked this reply of Srijan-da's, but what he said next was the usual, 'He's my cousin's childhood friend.'

Everything that Srijan-da and I had—the gardens we made, the conditions we set—was a relationship we had built ourselves. I hadn't been in touch with his cousin in years. Why did he have to introduce me as his cousin's friend? He could have just said I'm a friend, if at all there was no name for our relationship. Then it occurred to me that perhaps these thoughts were pointless, it wasn't as though everyone must give a considered and measured reply to every question.

Now the woman asked, 'How long have you known each other?'

'Since childhood,' I replied, 'it's been seventeen years.'

'That's so-o-o sweet.'

Srijan-da corrected me. 'Since his childhood. I was much older then.'

That's true. I remembered now, I was twelve then, a mere student of Class Seven. And he was in Class Eleven, already so well built at sixteen—while I still went to school in shorts.

He had told me his name even before I held the toy stethoscope to his chest. 'Srijan.'

Ever since, every time I ran into Srijan-da at their house, I would avoid his eyes, lose my voice, and so on. Stealing covert glances at him, or going up to his door on the pretext of looking for Chikan—these were the things I'd do, although there was no reason to hide anything. I didn't even understand everything then. And sometimes when he wasn't in his room, I would pick his clothes up from his bed and examine them. Once he had come in unexpectedly and asked, 'Want anything?'

'My pen's run out of ink. Chikan said your pen is on your bed.'

'Srijan-da doesn't keep his pen on the bed—that's the place for the pen,' he had pointed at his desk, feigning seriousness.

Snapping his fingers in front of my eyes, Srijan-da said, 'Which world have you gone off to? We have to order dinner, don't we?'

I returned from the flashback. The mischievous boy from seventeen years ago seemed to have become quieter now.

When the waitress asked whether we'd like to try some French wine, an answer slipped off my tongue, 'Chardonnay.' Promptly I remembered someone who used to love Chardonnay, someone I'd never seen but only heard. Did Srijan-da remember her too? Correcting myself, I said, 'No, let's try Sauvignon Blanc.'

'The French food here has no resemblance to what we ate in Pondicherry,' I told Srijan-da.

'What's weird is that you were expecting a similarity.'

That's true. I had thought of Pondicherry as a sort of miniature France, but in fact they had nothing in common. The crepes tasted different, so did the wines. There we had coastal heat, here, a debilitating cold.

'Remember how many replicas of the paintings from the Louvre they had put up at the restaurant in Pondicherry to prove themselves purebred French?'

'I don't remember anything, honestly.'

It was true Srijan-da hadn't made me agree to any conditions this time, but I was trying to unofficially follow the earlier ones. So, no discussions about the past, future or other people. And as for the condition of not loving, it was meant to be forever. I understood from Srijan-da's clipped, dry responses that we shouldn't be talking about the past.

A thought occurred to me: was it possible he looked at each episode of life as a self-contained compartment in a local train from bygone days—where you couldn't move from one coach to another? Where the passengers in each coach had their own world, their own things to talk about, where the stories from one compartment didn't travel to another. And even when a passenger from one coach happened to enter another one, their mouths were zipped.

He left it to me to decide what we'd have for dinner. Who doesn't like being in control of the situation? It was natural to like it. The Srijan-da I had seen in my adolescence didn't like giving up control to anyone else. In Pondicherry I had seen it change a little, now I saw it had changed a lot more.

After leaving the restaurant I took his hand and tried to lead him into a lane. Freeing himself, he said, 'Your gloves are so rough, Mallar.'

He seemed used to the cold, he didn't have gloves on. I had practically wrapped myself in a sack. I took my gloves off and held his hand. With a smile he said, 'Can't you do without making Srijan-da suffer with the touch of your ice-cold hand?'

I let go.

We bought ice cream. I was gazing at him eating his cone, his eyes, his lips, the small smear of ice cream on his nose.

'How can anyone eat if you look at them like that, baby? Mustn't stare at people when they eat.'

He was right. I was shameless. But then, I saw no reason for reserve and courtesy with Srijan-da.

The streets of Le Marais were magical by night. Even in this developed country, there was fear of thieves and pickpockets at this hour, especially in the deserted nooks and crannies. I spotted a handsome, attractive man, with a neatly styled brown beard and a little kohl in his eyes. In a turban and robe, he'd have looked exactly like a biblical character in one of the paintings adorning the walls of the Louvre. I couldn't tell whether he was a European, a Persian or an Arab. He was signalling to me, wanting to say something.

'Turn your eyes away and come into this lane on the right.'

'Are you jealous because I'm not looking at you?'

'It's not jealousy or anything, Mallar, Srijan-da is no longer at the age where people get jealous. Didn't your grandma tell you stories about kidnappers? Who put you in sacks? He'll lure you away the same way.'

'Is he a sex worker?'

'As if I'm a policeman who knows what each of the people here is up to.'

'Hmm.'

'I'm sure he is, that's what he looked like.'

'I see you're quite well up on things.'

'I've been in Paris a while, you know.'

A short distance away from the bustle of the bars and restaurants of Le Marais was the promenade by the Seine. There were benches here to sit on.

'You seem to be growing a paunch,' I said, half-asleep with my head in Srijan-da's lap.

'A good thing too, you're getting a free pillow on the bench.'

I had almost fallen asleep when Srijan-da woke me up with a gentle slap on my face, saying, 'This isn't Pondicherry, baby, men here don't sleep with their heads in other men's laps.'

'France is one of the most liberal countries in the world. Didn't you see men kissing so sweetly in Le Marais.'

'They kiss on the streets, they do lots more, but they don't sleep with their heads in other men's laps.'

I wish I understood. Maybe the men here like kissing each other in full view of people, but they don't know the peace that comes from hiding your face from the world in someone's lap.

'Let's go, if we stay on the bench any longer, people will think we're homeless.'

'Let them, people like me don't have homes anyway.'

'Enough of speaking in riddles, let's go now.'

Srijan-da was going to spend the night in my hotel because his guesthouse was a long way away. My hotel was right here in Le Marais.

'What're you looking at?' asked Srijan-da.

'The Louvre.'

'How do you mean?'

'You're the art, I'm the artist.'

Placing a bolster pillow in the middle of the bed, Srijan-da said, 'That's your side, this is mine. No man's land in the middle. All right?'

I didn't understand. Drawing the blanket up to his chest, Srijan-da fell asleep. We were on different sides of the bed but under the same blanket, with a pillow between us. Srijan-da was sleeping with his face turned away from me and I was trying to draw the map of a meandering river on his back. 'I'm exhausted after all the walking we did,' came the response. 'Let me sleep, don't disturb me.'

I tried to stroke his hair into place. He covered his ear with the bolster. With his face tucked beneath the pillow, he said, 'Didn't I say I'm tired, boy? If you trouble me any more, I'll go and sleep in the hotel lobby.'

It might seem he had begun to hand over control to others these days, but that wasn't actually the case. I knew it wasn't exhaustion, it was something else.

There were conditions, of course. There were lines between us, but those were by day—there were no barriers in the darkness of the night. Now the excuse for not letting me take his hand was my rough gloves. And there had never been a rule against looking into his eyes. Many years ago, there was a time when I knew that all our restrictions were for the world at large. When the world outside was wiped out, that gap between us melted away. When we were far from people, our bodies needed no cover. This cover was new.

Random thoughts coursed through my mind as I lay with my back to him. I had the urge to say, *The Paris Métro runs till midnight, you could have gone back to your guesthouse.* And then I scolded myself, *But why can't he come to my room just to sleep? Why can't he spend the time together as a friend?*

I left the bed and went to the bathroom. The mirror loved me even when no one else did. I gazed into it, placing the 'baby' from eleven years ago beside the Mallar of today. Who's the fairest of us all? I asked the mirror. The mirror didn't provide any undesirable answers. I examined myself closely. No, I hadn't become old. *Why are you judging your beauty by the others' standards? One doesn't quantify beauty. You're not supposed to weigh the flowers you offer the gods.*

Before going back to bed, I surveyed the street outside through the window. The bearded young guy with kohl-lined eyes from Le Marais was still hanging around, restlessly exhaling cigarette smoke. He was in search of either a customer or a companion for the night. Or perhaps he enjoyed roaming around the streets at night.

4

I'm sitting in the dilapidated outhouse of Srijan-da's home—his family home, that is. It's pitch dark. When they were affluent, the outhouse used to be occupied by servants, but now it has fallen into disrepair. I don't know why I'm sitting here. I can see Srijan-da's room from here, perhaps it's him I'm waiting for. The light's on in his room, he might be studying. The light goes out, I think he'll come out now. But the light goes on again, and then goes out once more. No one approaches the outhouse. The darkness in his room, the darkness in my outhouse, and between them a darkness even more dense—still, silent, wordless. I keep expecting someone to emerge from the darkness. Perhaps footsteps will break the silence, there will be a movement in the still air as someone walks through it. None of this happens.

Then a splash of water. Someone was splashing water on my face. And a horrible light. I wouldn't even be allowed to sleep in peace, I would have to open my eyes. I found Srijan-da splashing water from his hair on my face.

'Wakey wakey, Goldilocks. Can't delay any longer, Paris is up and running.'

'Is this any way to wake someone up?'

'What would you prefer? Morning ragas on the harmonium?'

I had an impulse to ask, *Don't you want to wake someone up this way every day, Srijan-da?*

The freshly bathed man was wearing a white singlet and the fragrance of jasmine—it was his soap. The sight made me want to hold him tight. He was moving towards the coffee table when I got out of bed and hugged him from the back. He didn't stop me. We moved towards the mirror in that pose, with me holding him.

'Srijan-da?'

'Mmm?'

'Have I ever told you how beautiful you are?'

'Now you tell me! You left it too late,' he said jokingly.

We were looking at each other in the mirror, at ourselves too. Standing on tiptoes, I nibbled his earlobe.

'Get ready quickly, the queue at Notre Dame gets enormous if you can't get there by eight.'

'Can't we see Notre Dame tomorrow—or some other day? It's not going to collapse if we don't see it today, will it?'

A few years later I heard the roof of Notre Dame had indeed collapsed, but that was a different story. If Srijan-da wasn't going to respond now to my nibbling his earlobe, he wasn't going to respond the rest of the day either. So I went off to brush my teeth.

In the bathroom mirror, I saw he had taken two shirts out of his bag, purple and orange, and was scratching his head. Still brushing my teeth, I said, 'Oyange.'

'What?'

'Wear the orange one.'

'As you wish, sir.'

There was a message on my phone from Shiuli-di. 'Happy?'

'Yes,' I answered.

'You're that heroine of a nineteenth-century novel,' came the reply. 'The type that can never forget their first love.'

Gazing at the ceiling, which was several hundred feet high, inside a gigantic structure from the Middle Ages, sunk in semi-darkness even in the dazzling sunlight, I reflected that this vastness seemed to have been created precisely to remind humans of their insignificance. Sunlight did enter, its colour transformed through the stained glass on which was etched a variety of stories and their characters. We went out of the Notre Dame cathedral, nearly three-quarters of a millennium in age, into the daylight.

I wasn't trying to hold Srijan-da's hand today. Let him not give himself to me if he didn't wish to. He began to hurry me when my eyes were caught by the shop window of a curio store, tugging at the sleeves of my blazer. When pulling me by the elbow didn't work, he finally grabbed my hand and tucked it in under his arm. Today his hand didn't have yesterday's stiffness.

Bored of Continental food, we hunted down an Indian restaurant. The menu was a mishmash of cuisines from the two Indias, North and South. Stopping at one of the items, I told Srijan-da, 'That flatmate of yours used to make such delicious Chettinad chicken.'

'You bet he did. He's a big guy now with his own start-up. Got the Millennial Entrepreneur Award too. I'm happy for him, I have an indirect contribution to his success, which he accepts.'

I noticed that this Ranganath was the only third person whom Srijan-da didn't mind talking about.

'Awesome! Do you still share a flat?'

But he didn't care for this question. He seemed a little surprised and was about to say something but decided to hold back. His expression conveyed to me that we were forgetting the conditions we had set. I had told Srijan-da I was a resident of Bengaluru now, but I didn't have the slightest idea of which city or street he lived in. Strange conditions, strange life.

From there we went to the Musée D'Orsay. This museum of modern art began where the last page of the Louvre ended. It held the art of the Industrial Age, of the past two hundred years. Interestingly, a large and defunct railway station had been converted into a museum, which was probably why the ceiling was arched, like the railway stations here. The paintings reminded me that once upon a time, I too used to draw—and not too badly at that. Why was I stuck in this corporate world?

Pointing out one of the paintings to Srijan-da, I said, 'Look how Jesus' twelve apostles are wandering around him in the nude, like angels.'

'Oh please, that's not Jesus, that's Plato. Of philosophy and Platonic-love fame. This one's called *The School of Plato*. Those twelve men are his students.'

'Looks like Jesus.'

'You're right. Maybe the resemblance is deliberate.'

'Srijan-da, I think in the third century, Platonic philosophy and Christianity set aside their mutual antagonism and began to slowly synthesize. Maybe that's what the artist was trying to convey.'

'Perhaps. Or it could even be that the artist intended to paint Jesus' disciples in the nude to show their love for one another. But in the age in which it was painted, two hundred years ago, people would have been furious at such a scandalous depiction of Jesus and his apostles. So Jesus was turned into Plato.'

'That's possible too.'

Art is a medium of expression, but you have to conceal many things to express yourself—often you have to conceal them specifically to express yourself.

Many people here sketched in museums. They drew sculptures, paintings, pillars, arches. The artists kept drawing while I kept looking at them.

'You used to pull out your sketchbook everywhere,' Srijan-da said. 'Would have been useful for you if you'd brought it here. You haven't stopped drawing, have you?'

'I do. Sometimes I feel like giving everything up and becoming an artist. And then it strikes me, what am I going to achieve as an artist? That's how life goes on.'

I imagined myself as a painter. Didn't feel like a bad idea.

'Mallar, come look at this one.' Pointing to a painting named *The Shepherd's Rest* by the artist Émile Bernard, Srijan-da said,

'Just like the drawing you made.' I realized he was right. A human figure in the nude, sleeping beneath a tree, with a shepherd boy keeping watch. His body was bare too. 'It struck me the first time I saw it, I thought of you.'

You thought of me! Even if it was because of a painting you saw. It feels good to know I have a place in your memories.

'I still have that sketch of yours, you know. But you never sent me that sketch you made on the Pondicherry rock beach.'

'You still remember it?'

'Shouldn't I? I remember everything I haven't got from you.'

There was just the one thing you didn't get from me—love—which you didn't want. I gave everything else unstintingly.

Was there any need to say these things? I reflected. *We'd set a condition of not loving. Why do you have to make me ride this Ferris wheel again and again? Climb and drop, climb and drop.*

The Ferris wheel we were on now was one of the world's largest. Roue de Paris, two hundred feet high. The two of us were sitting on it. A Ferris wheel ride is pretty interesting—when you're going up, everything on the surface of the earth seems small and insignificant. This pride is shattered on the way down. When you're going up, your blood pressure, anxiety, excitement—everything rises quickly, which is great fun. But every time you go up, you come down too. The elation of getting high and the disappointment of climbing down hit you by turns. Srijan-da made me ride this Ferris wheel of love and unlove every time, and brought me down to earth. Up and down, every time.

Srijan-da had very sharp eyes. He calmed my anxiety during the ascent with a firm look and a tight grip on my hands, then savoured my fear during the descent with mischievous glances and a grin. That devilish smile of his when he saw my fear was all too familiar. No matter how tight the race between emotion and apprehension was, Srijan-da knew when to rein the horse in—his own as well as the other person's.

We got off the Ferris wheel. I was so giddy I could have fallen. But I managed to keep my balance as we strolled along the Seine promenade. Srijan-da could make out the state I was in, and was enjoying himself with an amused smile. He had dragged me by my hand before getting onto the Ferris wheel, but he wasn't doing it now, simply for fun. Suddenly he jerked me away by the arm.

'Come this way.'

I couldn't tell what we were running away from, or whom.

'See that Indian there? My colleague.'

'But why are we running away from him?'

'Nasty guy. My project lead. Asks for updates whenever he sees me.'

'I've heard France's labour laws make it illegal to ask for updates outside office hours.'

'That's right, but the law applies to email only. It doesn't work when you meet face to face.'

'Hmm.'

'And besides, he follows Indian labour laws.'

'Hmm.'

'Hmm what?'

'Just say you're embarrassed to be seen with me.'

'Not at all,' Srijan-da said calmly. 'Srijan-da isn't afraid of anyone.'

'Prove it.'

'How?' Srijan-da stood with his hands on his hips, confidence written all over his face.

'A French kiss in France. Here on the bridge over the Seine.'

'Dream on!'

My God, I hadn't expected this. He actually dragged me to the middle of the bridge.

'Give me your lips . . . no, not like Donald Duck . . . Properly.'

And then? I held my lips out, and he thrust his thumb between us, literally giving me a thumbs down and running away.

I looked up at the sky to find the clouds parting. Srijan-da had been stiff yesterday, even this morning, but he was in a good mood now. He was like the damp and rainy Paris weather. After two gloomy days, we had a bright sun today in the sky. And in Srijan-da's heart. How long would it last? Paris was a city of great uncertainties, there was no knowing when it would change.

5

'You get me to agree to some condition or the other every time. Aren't you going to do it this time?'

We were sitting again on a bridge over the Seine. I'd tried a stronger liqueur today—grappa. Perhaps this was why I was speaking a bit incoherently.

'Baby loves conditions, isn't it?'

I had made him lie down on the bench and was running my fingertips across his stubble. After a pause he said, 'I've set a condition for myself, I won't tie you down with another. You must fly, and maybe seeing you fly will make me flutter my wings too. If you stop flying, my wings won't even exist.'

I could make no sense of this. A single grappa each couldn't have got us so drunk that his words and my ability to understand them should both have been badly affected. I was about to ask something when he held his finger up with the air of placing it on my lips to shush me and said, 'Quiet. No one comes to the Seine at night to chatter.'

He was always wrapped in mystery, but now he seemed to be surrounded by an unscalable wall.

I tried to understand why Srijan-da looked glum, why it seemed he hadn't got all he wanted, and hadn't wanted all he'd got. But asking too many questions would mean breaking our unwritten pact. Sometimes I wondered whether I'd made a mistake in not visiting him when he'd asked me to come over after his wedding with Shilpi was called off. And then I would reason in my own defence, how could I have changed the destiny of a man without knowing his wishes for tomorrow, a man whose past and future I was forbidden from asking about? If everything could be achieved from the present, why would our grammars even have included the other tenses?

Later that night, Srijan-da was leafing through a magazine on the sofa. His eyes were still, detached. The magazines in hotel rooms carried nothing but ads. What was he reading in those pages? I knelt in front of him and slowly took his hands.

'Let go, I want to sleep.'

I dragged him from the sofa and made him sit on the bed almost by force.

'Don't misbehave, I'm tired.'

I knocked him down into a lying position. He was holding on to the sheets, I took his hands and switched off the table lamp.

'I'm going to draw a map. Mountains, forests, ravines, plains— the river will pass through all of these. Sometimes rapid, sometimes slow, sometimes a cascade, sometimes still. Sometimes a whirlpool, sometimes the notes of a rain xylophone, sometimes deep in a canyon.'

I was flowing like a mountain stream. But no river can moisten all the earth it passes over. I could clearly tell his arms were stiff. Keeping his limbs and muscles and nerves rigid meant he was saying no. Both verbally and with his unyielding body.

But when the limbs and muscles and nerves were relaxed, did that mean yes? When my lips and nose flowed over his beard and neck, even his arms began to turn limp. To me this limpness was consent.

Cleverly, I let go of his hands. Because I could tell from his relaxed arms that now his body was saying yes, no matter what his lips uttered. The hammering of the heart, the profuse perspiration, the slackness in the muscles, the heightened breathing—none of this could lie, no matter what he said.

I knew this body, whether or not I knew the man. I understood the contrast between the refusal in his stern look and the plea in his large eyes. Having let go of his hands, I was gazing into his eyes. Even when you've actually released someone's hands, they continue to feel shackled from the tight grip you had on them before. I knew this sensation of being chained—from first-hand experience.

We seemed to be standing where there was no wind, waiting for a cyclone. But humans couldn't conjure up storms. Now he placed his palm in mine. The stilled afternoon wind suddenly began to rage. A tempest was devouring my river. Srijan-da uttered only a single word, 'Come.'

I became the river that merged with the turbulent ocean waves.

6

My arms and legs are tied. Once again I'm sitting in the outhouse of Srijan-da's family home, but I have no idea why I'm trussed up. Yet Srijan-da isn't here, he's far away in his own room with the lights switched on. I simply cannot tell why he has tied me up. If he doesn't actually want me close—if he wants me to keep my distance, why tie me up, why not set me free?

I woke up with a start. No, there was nothing to be afraid of.

Srijan-da was nestled next to me, almost smothering me—perhaps that was the reason for the weird dream. I tried to ease his weight off me, but it wrapped itself around me tighter. Slowly I extricated myself. The window curtains were parted, I went to draw them. The city lights falling on Srijan-da's uncovered back had created a magical sight. I didn't draw the curtains after all, I didn't need impenetrable darkness. I began to row along the stream of his back again. A little light was necessary to guide the boat, it was coming in through the window. I saw the stream wasn't exactly still, there were waves on it. All of a sudden, Srijan-da grabbed my hand in his sleep.

The morning brought a disconsolate face again. Srijan-da's, not the sky's.

'You're grown up now, Mallar, you have to understand these things. You have to listen if someone says no.'

I realized he was putting me in the dock. I knew of no better response than silence. But when he repeated himself, I said, 'It was you who gave in eventually.'

'What could I have done? I'm not used to saying no easily. And I've never said no to you.'

Not used to saying no? There was never any need to say no—such was the condition you tied us down with. The kind of condition that stopped me from thinking of you as anything but a body. It was always you who controlled when it would be yes and when no. These days you pretend you have handed over control to others, but that's only to protect your image. And your willingness or unwillingness to give yourself to me are all momentary impulses that come and go. And when they go, I'm irrelevant to you.

'Anyway, what's done is done,' Srijan-da said. 'I don't want to spend the rest of the day having a tiff with you. I think we're losing our cool because we haven't had breakfast. Let's get some coffee.'

On the way to a cafe, Srijan-da said, 'It may not be your fault, maybe the grappa last night was too strong.'

Is it essential to blame someone or something, I said in my head. *It's either my fault or the grappa's—the responsibility always has to be passed on to someone or something else. But why?*

After we had ordered coffee, Srijan-da went to the washroom, and then he got a call. Signalling to me, he went outside. I could see him through the glass window, talking busily. Checking my own phone, I found Shiuli-di had called. I called her back and said, 'You know, when he used to boss me around that was probably better. Now it seems he just submits himself to others, so that he has no responsibility, no need to justify anything to himself. When he lets the grappa take over, it's the fault of the grappa. When he lets me take over, it's my fault.'

'Got it.'

'He used to race through life earlier, now he walks on tiptoe. He used to order everyone around in the past, now he waits for a chance to be led in one direction or another by someone else, so that he can just drift along without attachment.'

Srijan-da returned to the table after a while.

Yesterday I couldn't tell why we were apart even though we were together. Today I couldn't tell why we were still together. But we were.

The smell of coffee is often a mood-lifter. There are many people in the world who can convince themselves that they're not guilty when put in the dock. I can't. I wouldn't have bothered if it had been someone else, but it wasn't easy to accept being labelled as the accused by Srijan-da. So I was trying to use the aroma of coffee to cheer myself up. Looking up, I found Srijan-da copying me, holding his cup up to his nose with both his hands, pretending to smell the coffee.

'I still remember how you like inhaling the smell of the food before eating it.'

'I see.'

'And I still have the pots you painted in my home in Chennai. I don't let anyone throw them away even if they want to.'

I looked at him in some surprise. It didn't take him long to read the question in my eyes.

'Let me tell you the whole story. This was about eight years ago. Baba called to say, I can't look after these plants of yours, you're far away, most of them have dried up, should I throw them away?'

'I see.'

'I told Baba, throw the plants away, just send the hand-painted pots to me in Chennai. I persuaded him to get a good packer to send some of the pots, or else they'd have broken in transit. I told Baba, don't worry about the expenses. The rest I took with me the next time I went home.'

And what about the condition that we cannot love? I didn't ask the question even though I was tempted to. 'So many things you've hoarded,' I said.

'I have to.'

'The pots are so old, the colours must have faded. You might as well throw them away.'

'I got hold of colours and brushes and tried to paint the ones that were fading. You know this isn't a skill I possess. After trying my hand at one of them, I figured I wouldn't be able to pull it off. So I told myself, let the colours fade, I'll keep the pots anyway.'

'Got it.'

'Even today, every time I look at the pots, I can see you painting them right in front of me. Even if the colours fade, I don't want the memories to be erased. Some memories you can only build once in your life.'

Do you like recalling the Mallar of eleven years ago? Then why don't you give yourself to who I am now? Am I not the same Mallar any more?

Srijan-da asked as we left the cafe, 'So what else can I show you in Paris, sir?'

'Anything you want to. Whatever's left I'll go see myself.' As if I wouldn't have got to see anything in Paris unless he led me everywhere by the hand.

'I haven't shown you the most important thing. The Eiffel Tower.'

Many of the shops where you can buy food in Europe are mobile vans. They cook the food right there and sell it. I found the young guy with kohl-lined eyes selling food from such a van. It was standing at the entrance to the field in front of the Eiffel Tower. He was wearing a T-shirt with the name and logo of the food van. He smiled at me when I tried to read the name. Fin de la route, it said, with an English caption below it, Your Search Ends Here. I was amused.

You cannot climb to the top of the Eiffel Tower if you haven't bought tickets beforehand, unless you're willing to stand in a long queue. So instead of climbing, we lay down on the grass in front of it to gauge its height. Rather than gaze at the minuteness of the world below from the top, it seemed more appropriate to respectfully acknowledge the huge dimensions of this manmade monument from below.

Lying on the grass, Srijan-da asked, 'Do you know why the Eiffel Tower was made, Mallar?'

'As a telegraph tower?'

'Nope.'

'Telephone?'

'Nope.'

'Radio?'

'Nope.'

'TV?'

'TV a hundred and thirty years ago?'

'Why was it made then?'

'It *is* used for radio and TV now, but it was made purely as a work of art. It was the tallest manmade structure of its time. Before it the pyramids of Egypt were the tallest. The Eiffel Tower was built to show the world the heights to which human creativity and technology and ambition and passion could reach. But there was no other use for it. It was built to be useless.'

'How odd.'

'Why? Then what were the pyramids built for?'

'The pyramids had a function. To act as tombs.'

'People could have been buried in boxes in the ground too, couldn't they?'

He was right. In every age people left behind a signature of the heights which their creations and achievements had reached, so that the next generation could build on it. For this you had to build not just useful but also some useless things. You had to rise above little temporary needs or urges and look much farther. These great structures were made to remind humans of their greatness.

'Do you know of the Paris Syndrome that many visitors to this city get?'

'What on earth is that?'

'When they get to Paris, many people discover the city isn't as beautiful as they had expected it to be. They go through a mental crisis because reality doesn't match their imagination. They heap abuses on the tour operator, weep over the fortune they saved and then wasted in Paris, or are plain disappointed. That's the Paris Syndrome for you.'

As for me, I found Paris even more beautiful than I'd imagined. Differences in perception are inevitable, but I didn't know something like the Paris Syndrome existed. The real-life version of colourful imagination was often drab, which was something I had probably understood during the twenty-nine years of my life. So while I didn't try to realize each of the things I had imagined, I never stopped being carried away by my imagination, and I never intended to stop either.

The sight of Srijan-da lying on the grass in the Champs de Mars park reminded me of a figure from thirteen years ago. A cloud covered the sun, and Srijan-da promptly fell asleep.

I speculated about what it would have been like to have been living with him. Would there be a lot of love, or would I have suffered from Paris Syndrome?

'What are you staring at?'

I was quite embarrassed when Srijan-da opened his eyes. How was I to know he would wake up all of a sudden? I wouldn't have been gazing at him if I'd known.

'Didn't you think even once during these six years that we'd meet again?' he asked.

'Of course I did. So many nights in bed I watched the blades of the fan go round and round instead of sleeping, imagining just this—that We've met somewhere, we're chatting. And then it would occur to me, there used to be so many conditions—now a new one was added—so the chatting didn't go very far . . .' Srijan-da gave me a sidelong glance, his expression full of admonition. I continued, ' . . . So I modified my imagination there in my bed. No conversation, but lots of feelings exchanged through looks.'

'Was that all you dreamt of—just chatting?'

'Yes.'

'Tell the truth.'

I considered saying, *Then let me tell you that I saw myself burrowing my face in your chest and crying.* But I didn't. You have to keep yourself strong in the presence of others. Srijan-da may have spotted the tear in the corner of my eye.

'Go on, Mallar, say it,' he said. 'There are no conditions this time after all.'

This was true, there were no conditions. Still I felt I had bound myself to some, whether he had mentioned them explicitly or not. Thirteen years ago too, he had let go of my hand, yet I'd followed him to the caretaker's room. I'd felt that though my arms and legs were free, I was tied nevertheless—someone had trussed me up with an invisible rope, bound me with invisible chains, to lead me there. Whether there were conditions or not, whether anyone wagged their finger at me and recited the rules or not, I still followed Srijan-da's instructions. I still kept the unstated limits in mind.

'Tell me, Mallar, if you'd like to . . .'

'No I don't want to. I have no desire. Just as well you had set the condition of not loving. Look at the state I'm in without loving. If I'd loved, I'd have gone mad.'

Rising to his feet from the grass, Srijan-da took both my hands in his, shook them gently and then arranged my hair.

'Sorry, Mallar.'

'I should say sorry too. Maybe I couldn't follow the conditions properly. Forgive me for the mistake.'

Srijan-da was still holding my hand. On an impulse I said, 'You know, eleven years ago, at the end of my holidays after I was done with school, when you were about to join your company, before you took the train to Chennai . . .'

'Yes . . .'

'You had insisted I shouldn't give you a farewell gift. No flowers, no sketches, nothing. I knew the weight of a sketch would be many times more than all your luggage. You didn't want to carry that weight.'

'It's just that . . .'

'And then for some reason you told me not even to go to the station. You were scared that I might say something or do something that would make all our promises irrelevant. Still I went. I kept myself as steady as a rock as long as you were there. Your train left, your coach disappeared slowly, I went to the tap on the platform and splashed water on my face for a long time . . .'

Srijan-da pressed my hand gently. I kept speaking. 'Who'd have known that not even all the water from the tap would manage to stop my tears? It might have hidden them, but it couldn't stop them.'

Srijan-da tried to put his arms around me. I said, 'No need, Srijan-da, even that day I didn't have to bury my face in your chest to weep. And now I've forgotten how to weep.'

He put his arms around me nonetheless, almost by force. I said, 'I gave my word, I kept it too. I didn't break the pact.'

Or maybe I did. Not revealing your suffering to the person in front of you is also love. No matter how miserable you are, not making the other person feel uncomfortable is also love. Considering I did give him that love, how could I claim to have honoured the pact?

'Maybe I've said too much. I was quieter and more docile last time in Pondicherry. Now I'm saying far too much.'

'You've always been quiet and docile, Mallar. Maybe that's why I'm so fond of you.'

The last stop was a glittering shopping mall. I bought some things for myself and some for my parents, while he bought a singing-and-dancing toy dog. A standing dog whose head, legs and body could be separated. It bobbed and nodded its head as it sang, rolled its hips as it danced. A fun toy.

'Who's this for?'

'Jhinuk.'

'All right. Who's Jhinuk?'

'Your classmate's niece.'

'I see. Never heard the name before.'

'Your Srijan-da's daughter.'

I locked eyes with him. I didn't know what to say.

'Juthika. My wife. Jhinuk has just turned three. They aren't here . . .'

I stood there, bewildered.

'At first I assumed you knew, later I realized you didn't . . .'

'That doesn't mean . . .'

I wasn't sure if I was angry. Even if I sought a reason to be angry, I wouldn't find one. Maybe I was feeling bad for Jhinuk and her mother. This was still plausible. But being completely incapable of judging which feelings were justified at that moment and which weren't, I decided to jump on the escalator and run away.

'Mallar, listen.'

'I won't. Let me go for now.'

No one in the crowd in the mall was bothered about what was happening. Srijan-da tried to force me off the escalator.

'Let me finish saying what I have to, you can go wherever you want to after that.'

I don't know what he wanted to finish saying, but it would have been best if the jostling as he tried to get me off the escalator had not ended the way it did.

Unable to hold his balance, Srijan-da fell on the shiny floor of the mall. Jhinuk's dog shattered into three pieces on impact. I felt bad, for this wasn't what I had wanted.

7

I held out my hand to help Srijan-da up. He didn't take it. He sat up but remained sitting on the floor. I sat down too. I picked up the broken toy meant for Jhinuk and tried to put the pieces together.

'I don't think you can put them together again, Mallar.'

One by one, I put the pieces together in my head—not letting me hold his hand, looking away, running away on seeing his colleague, the strange exchange about flying, avoiding the question of whether he shared a flat with Ranganath, putting the pillow as a barrier between us, and eventually blaming me and the alcohol for the barrier being broken.

Srijan-da was sitting very quietly on the floor. I wasn't worked up either. Srijan-da hadn't lied, since I hadn't asked any questions. And I hadn't asked because of the unwritten rule between us of not asking about the past, future, or other people. I might have had reason to be angry, but I couldn't have laid a claim to anything. Only one person could, and that was Jhinuk's mother. The trouble is that we want to love unconditionally, but then we want to set conditions too. I would have had to say goodbye to Srijan-da one day, I'd done it once already. But not this way. Not by levelling accusations at each other.

I put the three fragments of the broken toy in the plastic bag in his hand. He went towards the escalator. 'See you,' he said, pressing my palm lightly with his. I don't know where he went. I stared at the escalator going up for a couple of minutes. Why, I didn't know. With what expectation, what hope? I didn't know. Had anyone ever come down the escalator that goes up?

Shiuli-di had asked, 'Why exactly do you think you were so angry?'

'Emotions are emotions, they can burst out anytime.'

'Was it because you were still looking for a lover while he had started a family?'

'That's not nice, Oli-di. You're rubbing salt in my wound.'

I did meet him six months later. In Bengal. I was in Birajpur for a wedding and was waiting for a bus on the way back when I ran into him unexpectedly. He was carrying a four-year-old Jhinuk in his arms. A sweet, naughty little girl. She was punching Srijan-da on his chest softly because he had taken away her lollipop. He passed me a toffee through her. It was nice to see them. Then Srijan-da told Jhinuk, 'Give uncle a kiss.' I said, 'No no, she might hurt herself on my beard.'

As Jhinuk waved her arms around excitedly, Srijan-da said, 'Can I tell you something?'

'Tell me.'

'Our Paris meeting wasn't a coincidence.'

'What do you mean?'

'I didn't have any work in Paris, I was posted in Geneva. Juthika and Jhinuk were there too. Paris is about four hours by train. Chikan told me you were going to Paris. Maybe he had found out from a mutual friend. So I took the train. Your social media updates told me where you were, that was how I got to the Hôtel de Ville station.'

I looked at him in surprise for some time. He continued, 'Don't be angry about what happened in Paris. I just wanted very much to spend a couple of days with you. Urges are urges, right? Let alone two days, would you have given me even two minutes if I'd told you the truth?'

I didn't know the answer to this. 'I don't know,' I said. 'Maybe I wouldn't have, maybe I would. I'm a very bad person. What would you have done if I'd given you two days even after knowing everything—if I'd said yes?'

Perhaps Srijan-da wasn't prepared for this question. I said, 'I have to go, my bus will be here any minute. I'll have to wait another hour if I miss it.'

BOOK FOUR

The Final Image

Still, forget me not, if you do think of me in time
And yet no tear forms in the corner of your eye.

1

It was the first-ever solo exhibition of my paintings. The number of buyers was nowhere near the number of those who came up to me with questions. Who knew the difference between imagination and reality better than me? But then when the crowd at the gallery dwindled, it made me sad—I was hoping to get some more viewers at least if not customers.

Even Shiuli-di had taken time out to come. I went up to her and said, 'There you are, Oli-di, we need more people. Can't you get hold of some?'

'Your day lover, night lover, weekend lover, long-distance lover, phone lover, video-chat lover—half the gallery will be filled up if you can get hold of all of them. What do you need more people for?'

'You say such horrible things. I only have one person in my life—you know it very well.'

'Is that the truth?'

'It is.'

Suddenly someone covered my eyes from the back with their hands. These were not the hands that touched me every day. But they weren't unfamiliar either. I knew this smell. But how had he turned up here? And how had he come to know of my exhibition? Without too much hesitation, I tried to free myself from the hands, although their owner resisted. I turned around and it was as I'd thought. Srijan-da.

Sometimes you have to make difficult decisions. Sometimes you have to give up things. I'd taken just such a decision when I made up my mind to quit my job with a multinational to become a freelance artist. Instead of complaining that nothing new ever happened in my life, I had taken on the onus of doing something new.

But after chattering all day long at the exhibition, it seemed to me that if I'd spoken as much at the job I'd quit, I could have sold a million-dollar project. After answering thousands of questions from viewers here, I couldn't even sell a puny painting. And such weird questions. I was telling Shiuli-di on the phone, 'You know what they ask? Why are your figures so peculiar? As though I'm teaching anatomy lessons in biology. And they ask why my works are so expensive. Artists work free of cost after all.'

'Not everyone knows the true worth of art, darling.'

'Why do you create so much abstract art? Of course, I'm illustrating children's books after all. And the most bizarre question—how can we learn painting in a month and produce art that will be auctioned for lakhs? They want to become Dali and Picasso overnight. So many questions, but not one of them steps up to buy a painting.'

'Don't be upset, you're bound to find an admirer.'

'Not that I regret giving up a corporate career. What I say here is for myself, not on someone else's behalf. Here I try to sell only what I consider valuable.'

Luckily Romil was spending half the day here taking care of many of the things. Without him I'd have gone mad talking. The thing was that if anyone asked me a question, I answered with great enthusiasm, whether it was useful or useless, meaningful or silly. I felt bound to respond. It felt like a question paper in an examination—the more you answered, the more marks you got. I had told Romil why. 'I have stories in my paintings, I want to tell stories through them. And I have to explain the stories to people.'

He'd said, 'If you want to tell stories through your paintings, why not let the paintings tell them? Why do you have to tell them yourself all over again? Let each one read the story their own way. Maybe you suffer from insecurity, what if they read the story their way and not yours.'

So taking on this responsibility meant wasting both time and energy. Romil was good at maintaining a balance. Whenever anyone asked silly questions, he fobbed them off with a sweet smile. And when someone asked an intelligent question to which he didn't have an answer, the same smile was his weapon.

He knew only too well where and how to use that killer smile of his. When I had proposed to him a few months ago, he had smiled the same smile. Having known him for about three months, I knew that smile wasn't good news, it was his way of avoiding questions. Romil was wise—since I wasn't someone to make quick decisions either, I needed time as well. That day we had decided to give it more time. We were still giving it time.

I discovered a half-familiar face at the exhibition. 'Hi, I'm Nisha,' she said. 'May I ask a question if you don't mind, Mallar?'

'We didn't have plans for media coverage today, though.'

'Oh, so you know who I am. I'm here today not as a journalist but out of personal interest. Of course I can't get out of the habit of asking questions.'

'Very well, tell me.'

'These days we have this labelling, this is queer cinema, that is queer art, this is queer politics, that's a queer novel. Is this identification essential?'

I wasn't used to giving interviews. Without much thought I said, 'Has it ever happened to you, Nisha, that you've promised not to love someone, but you've had to hide your love away all the time? And because of this, you've lied to the other person every day? Even if you haven't done anything like this yourself, has someone done it with you?'

Nisha seemed to be taken aback by my question. She said, 'Promising love and cheating on me, lying to me—this has happened. But so far as I know, the opposite has not.'

'My stories are topsy turvy, you know. This is why it's important to point it out to everyone. That's why without queer art or queer literature, no one will get to know these stories.'

'I see. Tell me something about your art.'

I told her whatever came to mind. 'I wanted to become an artist to give a real form to some things I had imagined indistinctly
in adolescence. As it happened, I did end up becoming one.'

Nisha looked at me in bewilderment, and then asked, 'Any
inspiration behind these paintings?'

'There *was* someone. I'll convey my thanks to the person I
owe them to. They're an incomplete story, someone who handed
over an unfinished image and left. I added more strokes and
became an artist.'

'Were you very angry with them?'

2

'So my little Michelangelo is himself an artist now.'

'How did you know?'

'We can talk about that later, but how come you didn't give me this big news?'

What a strange man. I had the urge to say, *Did you give me all the big news in your life?*

'I saw it in the papers and came from Chennai.'

'But I didn't have it covered in the papers there. Did you see it on the Net?'

'No, let me tell you how it happened. One of my colleagues was in Bengaluru, he returned with some temple food, it was wrapped in a newspaper. Last Sunday's. I found your photo in it. The day before yesterday. And your exhibition ends tomorrow. So I drove all the way from Chennai today.'

When he saw my eyes moving about in search of someone or something, Srijan-da said without being asked, 'Juthika's busy this weekend, she couldn't make it. Jhinuk said she'd stay with her mother.'

I said, 'I hope I'll get to meet Juthika someday.'

I didn't know whether it was a genuine hope. Nor did I know what I'd say to her.

I introduced him to Romil. 'This is Srijan-da.'

'Oh, he's never told me about you. Do you live in Bengaluru? Let me show you around the exhibition.'

My ears were a little too sharp, I could hear the entire conversation.

'I knew from the way he used to draw in childhood that he'd be a great artist. I used to call him Michelangelo as a joke.'

'He'd rather be Van Gogh than Michelangelo though.' God alone knows when I told Romil this.

'But he went mad, didn't he?'

The exchanges were making me laugh.

'That's true. Come, let me show you the best painting in the exhibition.'

I heard Srijan-da's comment when he saw it. 'Very unfair.'

'What's unfair?'

'The Sold sticker. How unfortunate for me that it was sold before I got here.'

'Let me tell you then that Mr Dutta was here today. He's a queer entrepreneur, also a patron of queer art and culture. He's the one who bought it. He's also made a request, you could call it a commission in fact. He wants a realistic version of this abstract work. An oil painting. Larger, life-sized.'

Srijan-da scanned the work carefully. Then he threw a sharp glance at me and smiled mysteriously. I wasn't in the dark about the reason.

'It's lovely. I get some of it, but maybe I don't get some of it too.'

I felt he should have got the whole thing. Romil didn't normally talk too much about these paintings, but in this case he seemed to be explaining it enthusiastically to Srijan-da.

'Let me try to elaborate, even though I'm not particularly good at this. It's called *The Body Painter*. You can see a man lying on a rock, almost naked. One leg bent at the knee, the other stretched out. The front of the body is not clearly visible. And look, there's a hand painting flowers and vines and leaves on his back with a brush.'

'An adolescent boy's hand.'

'Yes, it's as though the boy has personally created this male body, and is trying to hide its nakedness with flowers and fruits.'

When I was young, I did draw Srijan-da's body and covered it with leaves and vines and flowers. And when our days of playing hide-and-seek ended, when I was commissioned to help with Srijan-da's roof garden, I had drawn with my pen and painted with my brush on Srijan-da's body. So his mysterious smile was far from inexplicable.

'Mallar had initially planned to make a realistic oil painting. It would have looked real. But that would have needed a model. Then he decided to make an abstract painting instead, without a model.'

'Not that the abstract one is any less alive.'

'Now Mr Dutta has commissioned a realistic oil painting. In fact he wants it larger than life-sized. Mr Dutta is a retired admiral. He's travelled around the world, and is the owner of a chain of boutique restaurants now. He pays personal attention to the details of the interior design at his restaurants. He's opening a new restaurant now, which is where he wanted to display the oil version of *The Body Painter*. It's a matter of great fortune to have such an important person as a customer and as an admirer. It's important to keep him happy. It's very important to do this painting with great care, because one customer gives birth to ten others, one admirer to a dozen more.'

'So you still need a model?' Srijan-da asked Romil.

'We do. We're looking.'

A little later, Srijan-da drew me to a corner and said, 'You seem very happy today.'

'Yes, with good reason.'

'And what is that?'

'Mr Dutta has given me an opportunity to do something interesting.'

'Can I say something, Mallar?'

'What.'

'As a child you'd never show me your sketchbook properly. But from what I saw, there's something I *can* say.'

'And what's that?'

'The model, the inspiration of most of the human figures I saw in the gallery was just the one person, isn't that right?'

'It is. Doesn't it make you happy?'

'Of course it does,' Srijan-da continued in a low voice. 'Of course I'm happy to know I proved useful to someone, that someone created so much art after seeing me. You know how people are still looking for the real woman behind the *Mona Lisa*? When you become Leonardo Da Vinci, they'll look for me as the source of your paintings.'

'What rubbish.'

'The newspaper report ran a painting of yours next to your photograph. The moment I saw it, I knew you still remembered Srijan-da.'

Forgetting wasn't possible. But I didn't feel like talking about these things either. 'OK' was all I said.

'I wouldn't be exaggerating if I told you it was that painting which drew me here. Anyway, I remember which ones in this gallery I posed for, I also know you drew the other ones in secret. I'm glad you did. But there's something I want.'

Who knew what he was going to ask for now. Not royalties, I hoped. Or would he plead with me not to tell his wife?

'Tell me what you want.'

'It's something that I want, and you want too.'

'What on earth do I want, Srijan-da?'

'You need a model, don't you?'

'I do.'

'So why not use the original model of that painting?'

I was surprised. No one agreed easily to this, not even all the professional models. 'Seriously?' I asked.

'Yes, Srijan-da doesn't say anything without thinking it through.'

I looked at him closely. He would be around thirty-four now. He'd worked out and maintained his appearance. Still a strong and well-built body. I said, 'Needs plenty of patience though. And you've seen the content. It'll have to be a bold painting.'

'That's fine about patience, I'll do it. And are you saying Srijan-da isn't bold enough?'

'Look, since the theme of the work is body painting, first I'll have to paint the model's body. This demands patience, it'll need an entire day. Then I'll take photographs on a DSLR and refer to them for my painting. But that doesn't mean I'll use the photographs alone. The model will also have to be present for quite some time.'

I could have painted the model and then painted fruits and flowers on the canvas, but the designs on the body of a life-sized model would have to look real too. They would have to sit properly in the folds and creases.

'It's essential to try new things in life, Mallar. Just like you gave up a stable job for a new adventure, I want to try something new too. I might as well try being patient.'

There were differences between a professional model used to such assignments and an amateur like Srijan-da. I had my doubts about whether he was up for it. And since this was a special commission for an important client, I didn't want to ruin it.

'I'm not promising just yet. I'll think it over and let you know in a few days.'

'All right, think it over.'

Srijan-da came to the exhibition again the next afternoon. He would drive back directly to Chennai from there.

'Well, did you think it over?'

'No . . . it's just that . . . I spoke to my gym trainer Bhaskar today. Talks have progressed with him, he's quite eager to do this. And besides, I also want to exhibit the photographs I take after painting the body. He'll get a portfolio too. He already has some modelling experience, the portfolio will help expand it.'

'I see.'

'He's agreed to charge a reasonable fee too.'

The fee was not important, but I had to give Srijan-da an excuse.

'I'll do it for free. And besides it's only talks, right, you haven't given your word yet. It's not a done deal.'

'You don't understand, Srijan-da.'

'Oh, is that how it is, baby? I'm breaking up with you.'

We broke up a long time ago!

Putting his hands on his hips, feigning anger with his lips, and smiling mischievously with his eyes, Srijan-da said, 'Is that how it is, baby? When you wanted, you painted the sun the stars trees forests anything you wanted on my body, and now? Srijan-da's body was a canvas once for your fancies. You think I'd have let you paint on me if I'd known this was what you were going to do?'

For some reason this made me laugh, and he laughed too.

I don't know why, but eventually I said yes. I felt everyone should get what's owed to them, so I might as well fulfil Srijanda's wishes. He certainly had both a direct and an indirect contribution to my becoming an artist. No art was possible without inspiration. The artist may not always have had a cordial relationship with the one who inspired them, but inspiration was inspiration, after all. Whether the artist owed it anything or not, they were always grateful for it. Gratitude should be acknowledged.

'Thank you, Mallar, see you soon. I'm buying just the one painting this time, next time I'll come with more time to spare and buy a few more.'

I didn't understand why of all things he picked the painting of fish to buy.

'Drive safely, take care.'

'I will.'

Packing up the unsold paintings after the exhibition, I wondered why he wanted to do this. He had mentioned the *Mona Lisa*—did he really want to be immortal like her through my paintbrush? Or was it some other reason that I couldn't fathom?

I heard footsteps among the boxes and crates heaped together. Someone came up to me and said, 'Hi busy man. Such a huge commission, I haven't yet given you a hug and said congratulations!'

With a smile I said, 'Say it, say it now.'

3

'What's the matter? You weren't expecting me?'

'No, it's just that . . .'

'Even the apartment security didn't look as surprised to see me as you do.'

I opened the door at 10 p.m. to find it was Romil. With a trolley suitcase.

'What I'm saying, Mallar, is we should start our trial period now.'

'I've been saying it for ages myself. But does that mean turning up on a whim at this hour with your bags . . .'

'You know very well I'm not one to plan.'

'You could have called. What if I wasn't home?'

'Mallar. What if this didn't happen, what if that happened differently, what if it had happened earlier . . . how long will these what-ifs go on?'

After Romil had gone to sleep, I texted Shiuli-di. 'Perfect,' came the answer. 'I'm very pleased you've moved in together.'

Silently, I told myself, *I'm glad you turned up without notice. If you'd given me the chance to make a decision, I'd have spent a decade vacillating.* I had the urge to wake Romil up and tell him this, but then I decided not to disturb his fresh sleep.

I found another message from Shiuli-di. 'You're apprehensive whether love will remain love once it turns into a routine of seeing each other every morning and evening.'

One-two-three-four . . . I was counting up in my head. And getting confused too.

'Are you tense about something again?'

Not at all, I was about to say. But then I realized it was impossible to fool Romil, and it made no sense to do so. There was a great deal of difference between love at night and a relationship by day. Everything was visible in the clear light of the morning. I was doing my Surya Namaskar routine in the wrong order—he had caught me. Shiuli-di was right, *You'll never be able to join the criminal profession, you're bound to get caught*. I didn't ask Shiuli-di though why I should go into that line in the first place.

'You enjoy seeing me tense—so I obliged.' I gave an evasive answer.

'Of course I do, I enjoy it very much. Some people look more beautiful when they're anxious.'

Pausing my routine, I shifted to the Shavasana, lying down flat. Putting his knees on mine, Romil said, 'Cool down. Now tell me what you're so concerned about.'

I used to be tense fifteen years ago too. Romil had caught me out now.

'Mr Dutta's interior designers suggested acrylic paintings for the restaurants, for an oil painting wouldn't match. But he's very keen on an oil, he loves classical art. My fear is, will it be appropriate?'

'Is this really what you're worrying about?'

'I have to take into account where the painting will be placed. What if it doesn't gel with the things around it?'

'The things around it are nothing but the things around it. I'm telling you, your painting will surpass everything.'

'Mr Dutta is very passionate. Both about art and about his restaurant chain. If he likes this one I hope he'll buy more paintings from me in future. You do realize how important this commission is?'

'I do.'

'He's also promised to connect me to the interior designers who work with him. He has an excellent network. If I can do the work well, I will have him as a valuable patron.'

'I'm certain you will.'

'It's very important to have patrons and good networks in this line of work. Earlier I used to think I'd get buyers from exhibitions and online sales. And those five-star hotels—they have superb paintings even in their bathrooms—I thought I'd go and sell my works to them. But there too you have to go through interior designers and architects. And I've found out there are hundreds of artists like me. Even the paintings in rich people's homes are chosen by their interior designers. Selling paintings is no cakewalk, Romil.'

'Right.'

'If it goes off well, if Mr Dutta is happy, this will be a milestone in my new career.'

'Got it.'

'Got what?'

'Come, sit on this stool.' Romil practically dragged me to it. 'What do you see, tell me.'

'A canvas. And an easel board.'

'And?'

'That's all. A white canvas, what else is there to see?'

'Listen to me. This white canvas is your starting point. Nothing but a white canvas. Forget all this rubbish of networking and patronage and interior design and sales—start thinking of your work as your passion, as your dream. The way you used to think right at the beginning. All the tension will flow away.'

'Hmm.'

'But whatever you might say, the model's a good choice. That cousin of yours will fit the bill, he's so well built. What's his name again?'

'Srijan-da.'

I'd told Romil earlier too that he wasn't really my cousin.

Srijan-da called at night to ask, 'How many days of leave should I apply for, sir?'

'I thought I told you already. Three days at least. On Monday I'll do the draft, partly on the model's body, partly on paper. The second day is for body painting as well as the photoshoot. On the third day, I'll start painting on the canvas using the photographs, but the model will have to be present. After that I'll use the photos to paint, I won't need the model.'

The next night there was a call again. What kind of colours would I use, how long would the colours stay on the body, et cetera? I said, 'I told you the other day. Usual body paint rubs off easily, so for this purpose one has to use paint that lasts a bit longer. But don't worry, I'll use good non-allergic body paint. You want to do something adventurous, and here you're worried about when the colours will go.'

There wasn't any response to this, however, other than two words, 'I see.' But the calls kept coming every night. The same subject. I told him, 'I'm busy at night, call in the afternoon if you must.' The response was, 'The questions might occur at night, right?'

I said, 'They can be kept for the next day, can't they?'

'And what if I want to hear someone's voice at night? . . . What is it, why have you gone silent all of a sudden?'

In my head I said, *You've tested my vulnerabilities earlier. Why do you have to do it again? Are you looking for some new vulnerability?*

He continued, 'Why are you so busy at night? Everyone else is busy during the day.'

Everything between us used to be measured out with precise. Whether in the mango orchard or in the roof garden, everything was like clockwork—when I'd arrive, when I'd depart, how much time I would spend there. Yes, it used to infuriate me back then, but later in life I admired the fact that Srijan-da kept everything under control. Why were we walking on an opposite path now?

'Can I ask you something else, Mallar?'

'Romil needs me for something urgent . . .'

'Hear me out for something not at all urgent. Won't take more than a minute.'

'OK, tell me.'

'You did paint those pictures with me in mind?'

'I was telling Romil yesterday that being an artist means suffering. Sometimes the painful things in life turn into inspiration.'

'What do you mean?'

'What do you suppose I mean?'

'Hmm.'

'And do you remember the conditions we had set? We're rummaging too much among future plans and past events. I'm sure you remember the most important thing—the conditions we agreed to.'

'Kids set conditions, Mallar. Grown-ups come to an understanding.'

'Meaning?'

'Nothing.'

I used to run a summer camp for the children in the housing complex where I lived. Drawing classes during the summer holidays, in my flat. The student who paid the most attention was Tuhin. This was recent, though, because he had joined the classes only because his parents had wanted him to.

'The dog seems very special. I don't think You've drawn anything with so much love before.'

'This is Kitty.'

'Lovely name. Your dog?'

'No, Trina's. My classmate in school. Her birthday is after the summer holidays. It's for her.'

'Whose, Kitty's?'

'No! Trina's.'

A smart twelve-year-old. He was making a pencil sketch to impress his classmate. Drawing Trina would mean getting caught, so he was drawing Trina's dog. I used to sketch on the sly too, but I wasn't as clever at that age.

It was almost time for Romil to come home from work. I said, 'Your mother will worry, Tuhin, you'd better go home now. You can finish the sketch in the next class. There are weeks to go, You'll finish it in good time, don't worry.'

No sooner had Tuhin left than Romil came in. Softly he told me, 'This boy will be your artistic heir one day. Such dedication!'

Being the artistic heir was fine, so long as he didn't inherit my fate.

In the evening Romil asked over a cup of tea, 'When is your cousin arriving, is it on Monday?'

'He's not related to me, I call him Dada only because he's older.'

In Paris, Srijan-da had asked why I still called him *da*. I'd said, 'I wouldn't have if you'd been my lover, but since you didn't become my lover, no harm addressing you as Dada. Besides, I also know people who call their lovers Dada. I find it very sweet.'

I went out the next morning to buy all the materials for the project. One by one, the shopkeeper handed me the bottles of paint. One had a woody fragrance, one had the saline aroma of the sea, another the scent of jasmine soap. I knew these were not the smells of the paints.

Back home I began to draft what to paint on the body of the model. The trouble was that no matter how much I told myself to treat the body as nothing but a canvas, I couldn't do it. *Think of his body as a model's, not as Srijan-da's,* I urged myself. *Think of the body as a canvas, not as that of a human.* But when the steed of imagination raced much faster than the jockey, reining it in was impossible.

I was making a draft so that the flowers and leaves corresponded to the creases and folds in his skin. So how could I eliminate the body, and how for that matter could I forget the person whose body it was? The draft would have to be made keeping in mind the curves, the lanes and by-lanes, the hills, the valleys of his body. Then I stopped working on the draft, having decided that I would do it with Srijan-da when he came on Monday. Imagining a person was far more painful compared with seeing them in person. It was all very well for Romil to have told me to begin with a blank canvas, but in this case the canvas was not a white sheet of paper but a flesh-and-blood person.

Srijan-da was calling. In the afternoon, in keeping with protocol. But I didn't feel like answering. I messaged, 'Text me if you have something to say.'

The answer was, 'I would have if it was something to be texted, but if I have something to say it has to be said.'

You can't respond to this. I didn't.

At night I dreamt I was lying next to a water tank on a roof in faint moonlight. There were many flower pots around me. They had patterns on them, and some had precious stones embedded in their sides, reflecting the light. I rose from the floor to walk. Gigantic flower pots blocked my way, I threaded a path around them. No, I wasn't exactly walking, I was circling, returning to the same spot repeatedly. Suddenly the darkness began to fade—I found colours all around me. Why so many colours? Dreams were supposed to be black and white. Why the discomfort in my eyes? I couldn't open them, someone seemed to have poured a heap of coloured powder on them. I was pleading to be allowed to open my eyes, but the colours wouldn't leave me, the powder wouldn't spare my eyes. I finally managed to open them with great effort.

I groped around the bed—why wasn't Romil here? A little later a figure walked up to me slowly in the darkness. Taking my head in his hands and burying it in his lap, he stroked my hair and said, 'I'm here.'

4

'Did I jump around a lot in my sleep last night, Romil?'

'Like you do every night.'

'Was I babbling?'

'As you often do in your sleep.'

Romil didn't say anything more. He only smiled his signature smile and left for work.

I had never lived with someone by day after spending the night with them. So I'd never had to bother about what I might have done or said at night. Mallar by day and Mallar by night had never had to become the same person. For some reason, Romil suddenly said yesterday, 'You've become much more tense since I moved in with you.'

I got down to a bit of yoga and meditation after Romil left. I had given my students four days off, or it would be more appropriate to say I had taken four days off from them. Meditation helped with anxiety, but where was the patience and concentration this needed? In the morning I felt the artist within me couldn't assert himself because I was treating the whole thing like a professional project through and through—perhaps the lack of harmony between the outer and inner Mallar was the cause for the disquiet. In the afternoon I felt just the opposite—I thought of the work as an outpouring of the torrent of inner joy rather than approaching it like a professional, which was why everything was out of control. Eventually, unable to contain myself, I climbed to the terrace and, hiding behind the water tank, let out a scream with the entire sky as my audience. A few crows flew away noisily from the top of the tank. I found some relief. Things like meditation were no good for me, this was far more helpful.

When I texted Shiuli-di about this, she wrote back, 'At first you were looking for an excuse to say no to him. Then when you said yes, you were trying to put together a logical reason for saying yes. Don't think too much about it.'

Anyway, the bell rang, and I went to open the door. Srijan-da had left Chennai at five in the morning, but he wasn't driving this time, he was flying. How had he managed to get through the Bangalore traffic and arrive so early?

'Coming,' I said pretty much at the top of my voice.

I opened the door to find Tuhin standing outside.

'Tuhin! I may have forgotten to inform your parents, no classes this week.'

'I know. I saw you were home, so I came over to show you. I'm almost done with the sketch. Can you tell me if it's OK?'

'It's very good. Come in.'

Old habits die hard. As usual I proceeded to make small corrections in the sketch with eraser and pencil. I know why people say I'm fastidious. Then I handed over the pencil to Tuhin.

'You have to bring some variations in tone to the face, or it'll look very flat, but don't make it too dark either.'

Suddenly something heavy landed on my shoulder. Both Tuhin and I were startled.

'How can you do that? The way you practically fell on me, the sketch could have been ruined.'

'Oh, I'm so sorry, Mallar.' And then, turning to Tuhin, 'Sorry boss.'

I'd forgotten to close the door. And both of us were looking so intently at the sketch that we didn't even realize someone had entered.

'Go into the other room, I'll be there in a minute.'

'As you wish, sir.'

As soon as I entered the room after sending Tuhin on his way, Srijan-da said, 'What's the assignment today, sir?'

'Go shower, here's a towel. I'll make coffee.'

'Canvas ready, sir.'

Srijan-da was standing in front of me. My canvas! My flesh-and-blood canvas! A body I knew, yet most of it seemed unknown. Conveying my thanks mentally to the physical frame that had made an artist out of me, I began work.

'Sit down on the stool.'

'Here I am.'

'Good.'

'What are you looking at?'

I was slowly circling the stool.

'Making a draft.'

'In your head?'

'The artist's first draft is in his head. And then everywhere else.'

I was ready to start. Right at the beginning I said, 'How will it work if you wriggle at the touch of the eyeliner? There's so much more to do.'

The first task was to draw an outline on the body with skin-coloured eyeliner. This was the first draft. 'I'll get used to it. Remember when you were a kid? I used to get angry when you drew on my body with a pen, and you used to get me angrier deliberately. After that you painted so many things with your paintbrush. It was uncomfortable, but I didn't stop you. What is it, why the troubled expression and creases on the forehead?'

I was in fact getting worried. What if he lost his patience? What if he couldn't take the pen and brush running across his body. I asked myself why I had picked someone new to this instead of an experienced model. It had never happened in my profession that someone had been able to read the anxiety on my face up close during work. This was a new experience. I set aside my worry with the thought that measured steps and prudence make art impossible.

'When I used to call you Michelangelo as a joke in childhood, I didn't know how right I was.'

'Oh really?'

'I got the chance later to see his work. I was in Italy last year. I saw *David*, I saw *The Creation of Adam*. He used to create male figures too, just like you.'

'Oh? Is that the only thing he and I have in common?'

'You like drawing males in the nude, don't you?'

'Shall I tell you why?'

'Yes.'

'Because beauty is naked, we hide our flaws with clothes.'

'I see.'

'What do you see?'

'What can I see, how much does an ignoramus know about art anyway? He can only pose. Can I say something?'

'Yes.'

'You still haven't shown me your sketchbook properly. You used to draw beneath the African tulip tree, and when you saw me, you'd close your sketchbook and run away in fear.'

Quietly, I reflected, *I began to feel grown-up from the day I stopped being afraid of you. But then there were new fears, and they turned me from grown-up to grown-old. I began to live with the fears that come from treading warily around everything, from taking two steps back every time I took one step forward.* But what I told him was, 'What's the point of seeing those childish sketches?'

'You won't show me?'

'You've talked enough, be quiet now for a while, this is delicate work.'

I felt I preferred the old Srijan-da who didn't rummage around in memories. Anyway, I made the drafts, first on his body, then on paper. I hadn't actually painted on his skin yet.

'Finally I can put on some clothes.'

'It will be much tougher the next two days. Be prepared mentally. Romil and I will make pasta tonight. Red sauce or white, which do you prefer?'

Srijan-da examined my palette carefully, then took a little red and put it on my nose. I realized this was his answer.

'So Srijan, Mallar said you were the model for the pictures he drew in childhood.'

'I was, Romil. Half the time I didn't know myself I was being drawn.'

The Bengaluru sky was clear tonight. We were lying on the roof, counting the stars.

'So unfair. You must claim half the royalties. He's still exploiting those drawings to make abstract paintings and living off them.'

I made Srijan-da's bed and went to the bedroom. Romil was reading.

'You seem anxious, Mallar.'

'Nothing major. Just wondering whether working on such an important commission with this man is too much of a risk.'

'What makes you think so?'

'He has no experience of professional modelling or of modelling for an artist. He's not supposed to have any, of course.'

'Don't worry, you're a skilful artist. He's not painting, you are.'

Still concerned about various things, I closed my eyes. Inevitably, they opened a little later. Even the sight of Romil sleeping peacefully was calming. That was what I was gazing at in the semi-darkness when he abruptly said, 'Hey, aren't you sleeping?'

'No. I wanted to look at you.'

'I know you do this often.'

'Why don't you open your eyes then? Why don't you respond?'

'Out of fear of this barrage of questions while I'm sleeping.'

I didn't know what I was babbling. It seemed a better idea to take advantage of Romil's waking up in the middle of the night to love him a little more. Which was what I did.

At breakfast Srijan-da asked Romil, 'How did the two of you meet?'

'Oh, that's quite a story. He was coming out of an art exhibition, his arms were piled with art equipment, he had a duffel bag hanging from his shoulder, he was about to lose his balance any moment. All it needed was a stumble. The poor fellow fell with all his stuff.'

'Oh. And then?'

'I picked it all up one by one and handed everything back.'

'Just like in the movies.'

'Exactly. His face was covered, so I could only see his eyes. They haunted me all of next week.'

'Full Bollywood! But why was his face covered?'

'Pollution mask.'

Finally I spoke. 'Enough of the made-up stories. Tell the truth now.'

Srijan-da looked at me in amusement and said, 'It's a good story, very sweet.'

I sighed, which Romil observed covertly. Then he said, 'Let me tell you the real story, Srijan.'

'Very well.'

'Have you seen the large paintings on the walls of Bengaluru? Graffiti. But you'll hardly ever see meaningful themes, it's mostly wild animals. So Mallar always used to ponder over how boring the graffiti was. He had an urge to make them more radical and revolutionary. One day he couldn't contain himself any longer and went off with spray paint to create some graffiti with powerful statements.'

'And then?'

'What do you suppose? The police caught him.'

'My God! Can someone like Mallar do such things?'

'You can't tell everything about a person from the outside. So the policemen ran with their batons, and Mallar with his equipment.'

'And then? Did you save him?'

Slapping the sofa loudly, Romil held up the index finger of his right hand. 'Correct, spot on!'

How can he fail to guess when you're about to spin such a predictable story? I silently pondered.

Looking at me out of the corner of his eyes, Romil said, 'Wait, let me finish the story. So the rest of it is the same as the earlier one. His face was covered, only the eyes were visible. Not a pollution mask, he's allergic to paint fumes.'

I sighed again. Srijan-da was grinning. Romil said, 'Oh all right, I might as well tell you how we actually met.'

'Tell the truth this time, OK?' said Srijan-da.

'I will. But sadly true stories are no fun, are they? We met on a dating app. He was passing my office, which I found out by the grace of GPS. But what turned out fortuitous was that I was going down the stairs when he took a U-turn after a couple of kilometres. He's never gone back since that U-turn.'

'Lovely!' said Srijan-da.

Romil said, 'What's so lovely? Everything in our generation happens through apps. Nothing interesting about it. Earlier people would meet so dramatically. Love would flower like in a story—there would be surprises, anxiety, fear, doubt, worry.'

Really? These were not very old. I had been in love the same way once, filled with surprises and anxiety, fear and doubt. I didn't want that any more.

Srijan-da said, 'Is that why you make up these stories?'

'No, it's just that I like creating plots,' said Romil. 'How did the two of you meet, Srijan?'

I was about to answer when I figured that the question wasn't what I thought it was. Srijan-da answered, 'Juthika is the daughter of a friend of my father's. So one day . . .'

Not particularly keen on listening to the story, I went into the kitchen to make toast. When I returned, the subject had changed.

Romil asked Srijan-da, 'I believe Mallar and you have known each other for eighteen years.'

'That's true. He came to my room disguised as a doctor.'

'How come you've never appeared to me disguised as a doctor, Mallar?'

The conversation veered around to Srijan-da's home and family. I had absolutely no interest in this, it was Romil who asked all the questions. I could see that now Srijan-da had no hesitation in discussing other people or the past and the future. Seeing me inhaling the vapour rising from the teacup, he smiled.

Jhinuk's school, Juthika's job, the new, larger flat they'd moved into—these were the topics of conversation. I even saw photographs of the flat on his mobile. The faded pots looked familiar. I saw he had remembered they weren't to be kept out in the sun and rain. Romil went into the kitchen to put the kettle on again. Since I was alone, Srijan-da asked, 'What should one do when the designs on the pots fade?'

In my head I said, *They're earthen pots, why not just break them and put them back in the earth.* What I uttered was, 'One should buy new pots.'

Maybe the response was a little too sharp for him. Still he said, 'Come and paint them again for me.'

When Romil came back from the kitchen, Srijan-da told him, 'Come to Chennai, both of you, I'm inviting you, I've told Mallar too.'

We began work after Romil had left for work. First I put setting spray all over Srijan-da's skin.

'What's the matter, why are you blinking? Did the spray get in your eye?'

'It did.'

'Liar.'

This was followed by a light moisturiser. Srijan-da was smiling gently, his eyes closed. Then foundation. Srijan-da threw oblique glances at me from time to time, but I paid no attention and tried to concentrate like a professional artist. I may not have become one yet, but I had to be one if I was to finish this project.

'Baby, the last time I saw these things was when the make-up artists made me up for my wedding.'

Back in my childhood, I'd told Srijan-da I'd do his make-up and dress him for his wedding. I pushed the memory away and focused on the work.

He was uncomfortable at the touch of the paintbrush, but he was dealing well with it. 'Why did you want to take this on?' I asked Srijan-da.

'I told you already, Mallar. I want to try something new, just like you.'

'OK.'

'Do you want a different reply?'

'No, I don't.'

'You really don't?'

'No.'

5

I didn't know whether Srijan-da was disappointed to know I didn't want a different answer, but unless I eliminated these thoughts from my head, I wouldn't be able to concentrate on my work. Still, I noticed that the patterns on the body were turning out well.

'Wait, I'll paint the next one with my fingers, it'll make you less uncomfortable.'

What happened was just the opposite. I didn't ask why he was getting goosebumps. But even if I didn't want to, it was impossible not to observe his responses from this distance. Still, I continued painting like a professional artist. Srijan-da was trying to restrain himself by closing his eyes. Now he opened them to look at me. I looked away and began to paint on his back.'

'Mallar.'

'Hmm.'

'Do you want a different answer to that question?'

'No, I told you I don't. How many answers can a single question have?'

'Ask me again. I'll give you a new answer.'

'What sort of silliness is this?'

'Go on, ask me again.'

'And what do you mean what answer do I want? Does the answer to a question depend on the expectation of the person in front of you?'

'Of course it does. The greatest realization of my life is that there's no such thing as the absolute truth. What the person in front of you wants to hear, what they like to think of as the truth, is the answer.'

'Is that why you create those make-believe worlds of yours all the time? New worlds with new conditions?

What was it that the cosmologists said? *Each set of preliminary conditions gives rise to a unique universe.*

'Of course I do. It took you so long to figure it out.'

'Hmm.'

'So go on and ask me again. Let's see what answer we get.'

'Just shut up. Keep your mouth shut as long as I'm working, you can have fun with your riddles afterwards.'

Not even once over the past two days had I given Srijan-da the thanks he deserved for taking on this assignment. On the contrary, I had been scolding him whenever possible. And he'd been quiet through it all. It wasn't supposed to be this way, Srijan-da had never been like this.

'Settle down quietly, Srijan-da, OK? I know it needs a lot of patience.'

Something came in the way when I was painting on Srijan-da's palm. I'd seen it before too. A ring. I had considered asking him at the outset whether he wanted to keep it on during the painting, but I didn't. When my brush went near it, he said on his own, 'Take this off, or the diamond will be smeared.'

I tried to remove the ring. He could have done it himself, I didn't know why he asked me to do it. His finger may have been slimmer when the ring had been made, so it took some effort to take it off.

'Put it in the bag, in that pocket on the right.'

I looked at the ring closely. It had a motif shaped like the number eight, the symbol of infinity. Perhaps it meant to convey that love is eternal, infinite, unending. I may have seen the ring in Paris too, but I wasn't particularly curious about it back then.

'My wedding ring.'

I'd asked Srijan-da to be quiet, and he had complied. But the constant looks he kept giving me—and those sighs! An intelligent man, Srijan-da, he could get his point across even without talking. He finally spoke up as we were nearing the end. 'Tell me, Mallar, what is this business of allowing time, testing things out?'

'What do you mean?'

'You and Romil, you said you're still testing things in your relationship, giving each other time, what does it mean?'

'Srijan-da, you and I always had an unwritten rule not to ask each other certain questions. So keep these questions to yourself.'

'So be it.'

'There are some relationships that give the right to ask each other questions—yours and mine isn't one of them.'

'Is that why you asked me to come? To arrive at an understanding without asking questions?'

'I didn't ask you to come. You came without being asked.'

It was proving difficult to create delicate designs when being bothered this way. I was trying to be sensitive to him, since it must have been exasperating for him to keep modelling without a break. Especially when confined within four walls in a state of near nudity. It was different for those who had experience with such assignments. Keeping these things in mind I had first completed the part of the painting that could be done while he was seated or lying down. And kept for later the ones for which he would have to stand.

Besides, I didn't have the patience of a professional artist either. And then all these questions. I had been living independently on my own terms for nearly a decade, so I was not in the habit of being questioned or answering them too often.

After a period of silence, there was another question. 'So Romil has no objection to your working with nude models, to your painting other men in the nude?'

I wasn't the first artist in the world to do this. If you looked at it that way, every artist should have a broken relationship, a broken home. I considered saying, *Don't see everything through the same lens of patriarchy*. But I felt it best not to give him a chance to talk too much, for which it was essential for me to keep quiet too. I could have given a sarcastic reply to the married man living with his family by dragging his domestic life into the discussion, but I didn't.

When I didn't respond, he continued, 'Or do the two of you also have the kind of relationship that, how did you put it, doesn't give the right to ask questions of each other?'

I said there was no reason for Srijan-da to lose sleep over these things. But this led me to another thought. On paper, Romil and I indeed didn't have the kind of relationship that gave us the right to question each other—as one would in a so-called marriage—and yet I happily answered all of Romil's questions. I should thank Srijan-da, I reflected, for making me recognize this.

I finished earlier than I'd thought. When I told him I was done, the first thing I saw in his eyes was disbelief.

'So soon?'

His expression suggested he hadn't expected the whole thing to be over so quickly. I'd have thought he'd be relieved at the test of his patience being over. Who knew what was going on?

Srijan-da used to make me work really hard on his garden. Some days it would infuriate me. One day he let me go early all of a sudden, which had enraged me even more. He was expecting a friend and had said, 'You've been working well today, take the rest of the day off.' His praise hadn't made me happy, nor had the unexpected respite from work. Srijan-da's expression right now suggested he wasn't too pleased at being suddenly released. However tedious it might have been, he seemed a little disappointed at the early end.

I got the DSLR. It was Romil's camera. Before taking the first photograph, I looked Srijan-da over carefully, looked at my work too. I was thinking about how, fourteen years ago, I used to sketch the same body and then cover it in leaves and flowers and fruits to conceal my desires. Today that body was standing in front of me with the leaves and flowers and fruits I had painted on it, not to hide anything but to express an artist's ideas. This body was a canvas of the heart, saying, *Paint some more on me if you like.*

'Wait, the photographs will come out better if I comb your hair.'

'All right, comb it.'

'I have to arrange the grapevines too.'

I took the first photograph on the DSLR. Then some more, in different poses.

'Are we done for the day, Mallar?'

'You'll have to wait a bit longer. I'm not all that great with a DSLR, I called Romil, he's just left his office, he'll be here in half an hour.'

'The photos seem pretty good. Why do we need more?'

'The photos he takes are even better. I want him to have a contribution to this project. He'll be here soon. In any case, it'll take time for the paint to dry, hang on a bit.'

'I will, but give me a beer if you have one. I'm tired.'

I got a couple of beer cans from the fridge.

'Catch.'

'When I visited the Vatican and saw *The Creation of Adam* one day, it reminded me of my Michelangelo tease from childhood.'

Patting myself on the back as I looked at Srijan-da, I told myself, *This is my creation too, I've created a man as well, this Adam is my creation. When God made man and leaves and flowers and vines, or when Michelangelo recreated the story of this creation, did these two great artists feel the same way on viewing their work as I am now?*

'What are you staring at?'

'At my creation. Perhaps my finest creation till now.'

'Don't forget there's a canvas beneath the creation, Mallar.'

The canvas is supposed to be covered by colours. But this one hadn't let itself be covered, it was far too living. I knew he was trying to present himself without inhibition, which I didn't want to see. It isn't easy for an artist to work with a talking canvas that asks questions.

'Wait, let me check who's at the door.'

Was the traffic easy today, or had Romil flown back in a helicopter? I opened the door to find Tuhin outside. He had something in a bag.

'I've nearly finished the sketch, sir.'

I found myself standing there with a beer can in one hand and paint on the other.

'Wait a minute, I don't want the paint on my hand to ruin this beautiful face.'

'All right, I'll hold it up for you to see.'

'It's lovely.'

'Thanks.'

'But it isn't finished. It'll look even better if the whiskers look sharper. The background needs shading. And some more shading to create a shadow to the right of the dog will look good. Leave a little space unshaded in the bottom right-hand corner, you have to sign there and add the date. Trina must remember when she got the sketch.'

I sent Tuhin on his way and went back into the room.

'I could hear you from in here. I'd asked you to sign and put the date on the sketch you gave me fourteen years ago. But you didn't put the year.'

'But you remember. Even though I didn't write it, you do remember it was exactly fourteen years ago.'

'If we're done for the day, can this silent canvas speak some more?'

'Allowed. But he must drink the beer carefully, it mustn't roll down the body.'

'Why do you think a flesh-and-blood person was so eager to be a canvas?'

Since he was so determined, he should be given a chance to come out with it. His honorarium for modelling.

'The artist won't talk today, let the canvas speak. Go ahead.'

'Baby, what if I tell you I wanted to redo the old garden and build it afresh?'

I had the urge to say, *You may have wanted to, but I didn't want it at all. In fact I wish I could get out of the garden of my childhood.* I had no idea whether he thought about everything differently because he was a married man.

But he wouldn't let me remain silent. His eyes were still seeking an answer in mine.

'I'm not saying I'm unhappy, Mallar. I have a happy life with Juthika and Jhinuk.'

I didn't know why he was telling me these things. I hadn't asked whether he was happy with his wife and child or not. Yet he went on, almost soliloquizing, 'I'm not unhappy, nor bored. These things can be fixed in Chennai too, I needn't have come all the way to Bengaluru. But I rushed to your city, not once but twice. Srijan-da isn't supposed to act this way, right Mallar, but why is Srijan-da behaving so crazily?'

I thought, *You rushed to my city? You rushed here for me?* Sipping his beer, he continued, 'We often imagine we're going to wring every single happiness from life. And we'll tiptoe around every single sadness. In the process, we forget the need to maintain a balance between the good and the bad. We only walk on tiptoe, we don't live.'

Was I the mud and slush on the road you were tiptoeing around? He went on, 'Srijan-da doesn't open up easily about these things, Mallar. But since I have a beer in my hand and words on my tongue, I might as well say them. Sometimes on my way to the office, I used to wonder where I was going, why I was going there. After leaving work, I'd feel I didn't want to go home, I wanted to be lost somewhere. I have everything, yet I feel I have nowhere to go. But Srijan-da has no reason to be unhappy. When you cannot find a reason for your anguish, it appears even more mysterious, even more unpredictable. There's no telling when it will come, when it will go, how much of an ache it will leave in your heart. And the unpredictability heightens the fear of unhappiness.'

'This can be treated, Srijan-da. You must have seen a doctor.'

'That's what I came to my childhood doctor for.'

All answers are not always useful. Maybe something was making him miserable, but I was not part of that atlas of misery, I couldn't fix his problem.

'This doctor doesn't have a treatment, Srijan-da.'

'Maybe he does. Because I see the doctor cycling towards the mango orchard. He doesn't want to let go of me. At times I climb up to the roof of our house and stand against the breeze, thinking someone will perhaps come with colours and brushes to paint on my body. He'll hurt me with his pen strokes and little by little I'll relish the pain.'

For some reason I felt he was telling me the truth. Srijan-da was capable of hiding the truth, of avoiding his obligation to tell the whole truth, but he didn't lie very much—I accepted this. I wondered whether something like love might have sprung up between us if he had said this a decade ago. And if it had, would it have lasted?

Taking another sip of his beer, Srijan-da asked, 'Do you consider Srijan-da a coward?'

I didn't understand why he was suddenly asking this question. Not that I had thought about this. As a child I would consider him brave. But trying to arrive at an answer, I remembered many other incidents.

He used to call me to their old outhouse. The rickety cot and damp room was our nest, our nook, our nuptial bed. Of course, everything was thrilling at one point in life. Other than the roof garden by day and, sometimes, the outhouse by night, I didn't frequent their house very much, and didn't want to, either. I was far too afraid—of Srijan-da, no, not exactly of Srijan-da, it was a different fear: of breaking my pledge, of doubt about whether he'd call me over tonight, of the pendulum swinging between hope and despair over whether he would turn up even after setting up our tryst. Sometimes I would open their main gate furtively under the cover of night, sneak past the shadowy trees to the even darker outhouse and wait there.

The devil's tree flowers at night, filling the air with its maddening fragrance. It was those flowers that adorned our nights. Caught between the intoxicating smell on one side and the sultry heat and mosquitoes on the other, I waited, my heart thumping in fear. He was here. But some nights he was so late that my eyes had clouded by then. Who knows, maybe he liked to see my eyes misted over, maybe he derived joy from weighing my fear. There were exceptions too. Sometimes I'd be angry enough to lock the outhouse door and sit inside. He'd knock on it, though softly, so that no one else could hear. Gentle, cautious raps, one at a time. Perhaps I liked thinking of the entreaty in that knocking as a declaration of love. Not all kinds of love leave room for hurt feelings, even less so when that love is not a romance. So I was forced to unlock the door. Did I have a choice? Now I feel I was rather bold, but at that time I considered myself a coward. Srijan-da shared this fear too, but he used to lock it away within me.

We looked at the floor in silence for some time with our beers.

'There's one thing I do feel guilty about,' said Srijan-da.

'What's that?'

'When you opened the outhouse door, I could often tell your eyes were dry from wiping your tears. I could tell, but I would pretend I didn't. I used to think I was compensating you for one kind of suffering with another kind of joy.'

How strange that we were thinking of the same thing.

'I realized it too. Why did you think I didn't?'

'Can I ask something?'

'No. You've asked enough, I preferred our days of not asking questions.'

'I will anyway. Why did you agree to my modelling for you after saying no, Mallar?'

This was a repetition of his earlier questions. Srijan-da didn't like taking favours from anyone for fear of having to be grateful, but he extracted a good deal—in a way that made it seem the giver was benefiting from his largesse. Maybe Srijan-da wanted me to feel grateful and thank him. Perhaps not just verbal thanks but something more.

I said, 'I felt I should convey my gratitude to the person who was the inspiration for my art.'

But what I told myself was, *I wanted to thank the person who enabled my artistic self to emerge by inflicting pain on me.*

'I have to make an online booking, Srijan-da, I need to use my laptop.'

'Go ahead, use it.'

I wasn't keen on prolonging this particular conversation, so I thought it would be better to turn away from him and look at the laptop screen. Still he continued, 'I've asked many questions, Mallar, just one more to go.'

'What?'

'The love we couldn't have then—can't we ever have it?'

He was probably uttering the word *love* after twelve years. The last time I had heard him say it was when he had set the condition of not loving. Luckily we weren't facing each other. Maybe this was what I had wanted to hear—not today, but years ago. I didn't want to hear it now. He had managed our not loving much better, this new love was too scattered and uncontrolled. All I said, 'Let me complete the booking.'

A little later, I felt the light touch of a hand on my shoulder, someone's breath playing in my hair, a pair of lips sinking into them.

'Tell me honestly, will we never be able to love?'

Perhaps this was the question you wanted to ask, the answer to which you wanted, but that was not why I had asked you to come. All I said was, 'No, I can't. I really can't. Let go.'

But he didn't. His lips were looking for an unlawful entry close to my ear.

'I put a lot of work into those designs. Don't spoil them. You and I don't have that relationship any more.'

Drunkenly he said, his words slurring, 'What relationship, baby? You and I had so much even without a relationship.'

'Those days are gone, believe me. They won't come back just because you want them to. Because I don't want them to come back.'

I wasn't looking at him, but on my laptop screen I could see a dark reflection that was trying to consume me. His lips were still trailing across my skin in harmony with his breathing.

'I know this is wrong. Blame the beer. I still want to love Mallar. I know I set the condition myself to suppress the love. I was punished for it too. I couldn't take it any more, that's why I came to you from Chennai.'

'I know this love. Love was forbidden to us, let it stay forbidden.'

I couldn't stand his touch, this love felt intolerable. I rose from the chair and went to the opposite corner of the room. But the painted figure came towards me. My creation was closing in to devour me.

The pillar of paint now embraced me.

'You know why I lied to you in Paris, baby. You also admitted it makes no difference to you whether I'm married or not.'

His deep breathing was unbearable. I said, 'That was a different time.'

'Why, because you're in a relationship now? Anyway, you're in an open relationship.'

So being in an open relationship meant I was easy to get? Just because my door was open for you at one time in the past, did it mean it was still open? The Mallar who waited behind that door was much more vulnerable. He's a different person now.

I said, 'That's our personal matter, not for you to be involved in. Don't touch me.'

But the contagion had spread already. My white singlet had splotches of colour. The paint from his hand had left marks on the bare skin on my shoulder. A powerful beast seemed intent on crushing me between his muscular arms and body. The paint had not dried on him yet. The more I tried to free myself, the more the colours spread all over me. I was trying to get away, but the pillar of paint had come to life and was holding me tight.

'I didn't come uninvited, Mallar. When I saw the coverage of your exhibition from Chennai, it seemed to me—and it became clear at your exhibition—that you hadn't forgotten. You hadn't forgotten Srijan-da.'

'I beg of you, Srijan-da, don't do this, all the body painting, all the patterns will be ruined. There's more to be done.'

'You've taken photographs, you can work with those.'

'That's another matter. But how dare you touch me without my consent?'

'You did the same thing a year ago. And does loving one person mean you can't love someone else?'

I had done it without knowing, but what Srijan-da was doing today was with full knowledge. But he was in no condition to see reason, therefore talking to him wouldn't help. When he tried to put his arms around me again, I had no option but to push him.

Srijan-da fell to the floor, and so did the three-legged stool behind him. The bottles of paint I had put on it fell too and shattered. Just like fourteen years ago, Srijan-da was sitting bewildered on the floor, naked, with scattered, misshapen patches of paint all over his body, and streaks of colour and shards of glass around him.

6

'Open the door, Mallar, I promise I won't bother you.'

Srijan-da kept banging on the door. I had run into the bath-room to hide, turning on the shower and trying to rub the col-ours off my body. I had soaked my singlet in a bucket, where the colours kept coming off and dispersing in the water. However hard I rubbed, the colours wouldn't come off my skin. I couldn't show Romil these colours, they weren't the kind of colours one would like. Neither the water from the shower nor the soap seemed able to get the paint off. Maybe there was no more colour on my skin, but it felt as though there was, and I kept scraping away with a husk. My skin was coming off from the abrasion while the hammering on the door went on.

'Mallar, I promise not to touch you. Srijan-da doesn't break his word.'

There would be a similar hammering on the door of the out-house. No, not similar, just the opposite, in fact—slow, almost silent. A banging on the door meant not to be heard by anyone else except the person inside. And it was this person inside who seemed to bear the responsibility to keep the sound concealed. I may have been the one to lock the door, but it was Srijan-da who seemed to have imprisoned me.

We'd have tiffs afterwards too. There was a huge tree with a hollow in one corner of the orchard. I would take shelter in it when I was hurt. The rain didn't relent easily in July—I'd stay in the hollow, waiting for it to stop. The rain outside and the rain behind my eyelids—both. Some days I went home when the rain stopped. On other days Srijan-da would appear, hold his arms out and ask me to climb down. Some days I was so happy just to see him holding his arms out that I climbed down on my own, other days I'd display more pique and he'd have to coax and cajole me before reaching in and pulling me out with his strong arms. Some days he would carry me in those arms to the pond and make me sit on its paved edge. But the days he knew I was only feigning my pique, he would dump me in the sludge beside the pond. Some days he rescued me from the muck, some days he smiled cheekily watching me try to rub the mud off my body. Then he would pick me up, take me to the pond, wash off every stain, all the time scanning my body for remnants of mud with the same impish eyes.

Today I didn't have a hollow in a tree to take refuge—my bathroom was my hollow. Getting the muck off had been easy, getting the paint off was not, so I gave up. If you felt you have some paint sticking to you even after you've got it all off, removing it was even tougher. I gave up because the banging on the door was not soft and gentle like it used to be.

How long could I stay in the bathroom anyway without drying myself? I had no choice but to open the door. There wasn't a towel nearby, and the singlet I was wearing was soaking in the bucket. So when I opened the door, I was still wet. My bare body was trembling—in the cold, in anger, in resentment. We stood opposite each other, almost entirely unclothed. But this was no moment of love. I was staring at the floor, not in embarrassment but to hide my anger.

Eventually, I lifted my eyes, without knowing what I wanted to see. Maybe I wanted to spot guilt in his eyes. The guilt of ruining my artwork, of painting my body in undesired colours.

Srijan-da had been trying to tie into chains me from the beginning. First the reference to the open relationship between Romil and me, then the attempt to get me to ask a specific question, followed by the effort to extract an answer, and then the story of his own weariness—maybe it was true—but when none of these worked, he tried to pin me down with his own hands, with his body.

I didn't want Romil to see this sight. Pieces of glass, paint and art material were scattered all over the floor. It was like a battlefield. We were looking at each other amid this. My eyes held discontent, and his, perhaps a hint of remorse. Water droplets were still falling from my body, and his had splotches of paint. I didn't want to show Romil this war zone.

The bell rang again.

7

Compose yourself first, don't run to the door at once, I told myself. Srijan-da held out a towel. I told him to dress, since all the designs had been ruined in any case. I put on clean clothes too, and opened the door only after the bell had rung several times. The pizza-delivery guy was furious.

Srijan-da packed his bag and brought it into the drawing room, where he picked up a slice of pizza from the table. Gathering several acrylics from my store of paintings, I began to dump them in a large cardboard box.

'What do you think you're doing, Mallar? The paintings will be spoilt. Why take your anger out on them?'

'I need to get rid of these memories.'

He may have noticed that all the paintings piled in the box had been directly or indirectly inspired by him.

'Don't be so heartless with them. They're your own creations.'

Calming myself, I began to arrange them in the box.

'Don't worry, I'm not mad, I won't destroy my work with my own hands.'

'Then why are you throwing them into the box? It's one thing to be angry with your model, but the paintings are your children.'

The children of our incomplete love, perhaps.

'I want to get them out of the house. I'll sell them—even if someone pays one rupee for the lot.'

Once I had boxed all the paintings I had identified as unwanted, I brought three sketchbooks from the cupboard to add to them. Srijan-da gripped my hand tightly, then loosened his hold.

'Are these the sketchbooks you used to hide from me in childhood?'

'Yes.'

'I'm taking them with me. To Chennai.'

'As you wish. I don't want to keep them. Take them wherever your heart desires, do whatever you want with them.'

Srijan-da put the sketchbooks in his suitcase.

'Please don't mind, Mallar, but the memories are not yours alone—they belong to both of us. They have to remain with someone. Since you don't want to keep them, I might as well take the responsibility.'

I smiled a bit, then said to myself, *Fine, you can take the responsibility. But you will never understand the pain of carrying them on your back the way I have. Time has eaten into them and reduced their weight.*

'I'll go now. Take care.'

'I will.'

As he was going out the door, Srijan-da looked at me and said, 'I hope I haven't ruined your project at least. I'm sure you can refer to the photographs and make the final oil painting.'

I said bye and closed the door behind him. The bell rang again in a few minutes.

Romil said as soon as he entered, 'So much traffic even at this hour of the afternoon. Show me what you've painted. Where's Srijan?'

He was surprised to see the state of my studio. Broken bottles, paint splattered on the floor, half my paintings missing— it was natural to be surprised. After some thought, he said, 'Is everything all right, Mallar? Are you OK?'

8

Romil's eyes swept around the room, taking in the debris. Taking in the broken flower vase, the pieces of glass, the sticky patches of paint drying on the floor. I avoided his eyes, I think he was avoiding mine too. He went out to look for something.

He came back with a broom and used it to gather the broken pieces of glass in a pile. I was terrified of broken glass, but Romil took care of everything. Fortunately, it was glass, which meant I couldn't put the pieces back together—or else, who knows, I might have tried to make bottles out of them.

Romil said, 'Why are you lurking in a corner? Come here.'

I went up to him. 'Relax,' he said, 'there's no glass on the floor. Come.'

There in the middle of the battlefield, he held me very gently, rubbing his hand on my back and saying softly, 'I'm here, don't worry.'

In the evening I saw a text, 'I'm not OK. Haven't been for a few days. Don't know myself what I'm doing.' It had come a few hours ago but I hadn't seen it till now. I typed, 'Maybe you aren't OK, but I'm not the treatment, am I? There must be other solutions.'

I deleted the reply without sending it. An hour later, another text. 'I walked around the airport for a long time, wondering where to go and why. The security people were staring at me suspiciously. Eventually I advanced the ticket to Chennai. I've just put on my seatbelt on the plane. Time to say goodbye. Don't know if I'll ever be back in your city.'

I didn't reply.

The next morning I messaged my students to tell them I'd resume classes from today. After calming down, I'd more or less decided to start afresh with a new model. I'd talked to my gym trainer Bhaskar earlier about it after all, and fortunately, for me, he'd agreed. Mr Dutta had also granted an extension. This could have given him a negative impression of me, but perhaps he'd understood artists couldn't always work to a timetable.

I had a chat with Shiuli-di on the phone.

'He always leaves the story in a mess, Mallar. What's new?'

'Who knows, maybe I became an artist by adding my imagination to those messed-up stories.'

It was true, the artist might pick up a lump of clay and let his imagination run, but once it had taken the form of the goddess, there was not much he could do. An incomplete story could be moulded into a form. You could play with it every day, build it the way you wanted to, take it apart, rebuild it. For all I knew, it was this habit of building and rebuilding every day that had awakened the poet in me, making me an artist. In exchange for the sadness, it had also given me something good.

'Don't stress. Sometimes you have to step back even after going a long way forward with something. I know you'd invested a lot of time and energy on this. Sometimes you have to forget even such large investments. Start the project afresh, everything will go well.'

'You know, Shiuli-di, the condition we had set of not looking back was a good one—it was a mistake to try and paint the past.'

'Can you tell me why you loved him? Was it because he wasn't available, because he'd erected a wall around himself, because every building surrounded by high walls feels like a palace? And then the illusion of his being hard to get vanished when he wanted to submit?'

'That's crazy. I never loved him. Don't you know we had set a condition not to love?'

'Can I say something?'

'Of course.'

'You kept playing the role of someone who didn't love him, he applauded your performance as a member of the audience, and you considered this praise the Oscar for best actor—that was your consolation. This is what happened to you, I'm telling you honestly.'

On a whim, I told Shiuli-di about Srijan-da's texts.

'I was right. You couldn't ignore the messages even though you pretended to. That's why you're still thinking about them.'

Shiuli-di was always blunt. She continued, 'People often seek the easiest solution to stay well. It's OK—if he takes a little initiative, he will solve his problem himself.'

My students came to class. Tuhin was looking miserable, he didn't say a word about his sketch. He got down to doing watercolours with the others and left before them with an excuse. After everyone had left, I saw him sitting quietly by the swimming pool, gazing into the water. I went downstairs.

'Everything all right, Tuhin?'

'We're leaving Bengaluru. Dad's changing his job. Hyderabad. Mum knew already. I found out yesterday.'

'When are you going?'

'Before the end of the summer holidays. Our school has a branch there.'

'Hmm, that's why you're sad.'

He took his sketchbook out of his bag, slowly tore out the page with the sketch of Trina's dog and gave it to me. I didn't know what to do with it.

'I couldn't finish it, sir.'

Not knowing how to respond, I said, 'You drew it so beautifully, why not keep it? Finish it later.'

'No, sir, you keep it. Complete it the way you want to. Put it up at your exhibition.'

'Are you sure? What if later you wish you'd kept it?'

I didn't know what thoughts went through his head, but he took the drawing back and tucked it into his sketchbook.

Silently, I thought, *Why, Tuhin? Why are you like this? Why this polite acceptance and adjustment at such a young age? You could have made a scene at home, you could have said you won't go. It might not have worked, but at least with me you could have cried a bit, complained a little. Why must you compromise? And even if the sketch is incomplete, you could still have gone over to Trina's place and given it to her. Maybe you won't meet her again, but why not let her know? Why accommodate so much?*

I didn't say any of this. Tuhin was on his way home when I ran up to him.

'Listen, Tuhin.'

'What?'

'If you really don't feel like keeping the sketch, you can give it to me.'

Taking the sketch out again, Tuhin handed it over quite nonchalantly before walking away. I thanked myself. It was best not to carry around an unfinished drawing all your life. I knew incomplete works were useful, you could mix in flights of fancy to draw and paint many more things. What if the painting were this way and not that, I could have added this, taken away that— an incomplete work was surrounded by the luxury of such possibilities. But it was best not to be immersed in such thoughts. Let Tuhin draw new pictures in a new city. His unfinished drawing might as well stay with me.

I came back home and put it away in my drawer, thinking, *I hope you never have to come back for this sketch, Tuhin. I am locking it away.*

'I'm starting work with Bhaskar tomorrow,' I told Romil. 'Delete the photographs of Srijan-da from your DSLR.'

Romil opened his laptop and called me over.

'Mallar, the photos are pretty good, see? What's wrong with using these as a reference?'

'It's not like you don't know what's wrong with it, Romil.'

'What if I say use them anyway? The final decision's yours, but I thought I'd try telling you.'

'Let me think about it.'

'The address of your painting is Mr Dutta's restaurant, not your home. Don't imagine it will pursue you all your life.'

I gave in to Romil ultimately, perhaps because that was what I wanted too. I might as well express my gratitude one last time to the person because of whom I became an artist.

An arduous project, but it eventually came to an end. Romil and I went to Mr Dutta's restaurant to install it. He was very pleased with my work, praising it effusively. 'How do you feel now that it's done, Mallar?' he asked.

'I feel a weight off my back.'

'You'll be here for the inauguration of the restaurant, won't you?'

'I have something important that day, may I let you know?'

It was late by the time we got home after dinner. On the way back, I discovered texts from Srijan-da on my phone.

'Why did you throw me out that way, Mallar? Did you want to be free of me?'

Next message: 'Or were you trying to wipe away childhood memories?'

I thought of texting that I'd just dropped off that final memory somewhere away from home, but I didn't. I wrote, 'After drawing something, we often wipe it away, especially when we have to make a new drawing on the same page.'

Srijan-da kept typing, 'No worries, all the memories are locked away in my drawer, in your sketchbook. Someday Srijan-da might want to see them again. Srijan-da will unlock the drawer that day.'

I didn't reply. He continued, 'You might want to see them again too . . .'

'Perhaps not . . .' I typed.

'Really? If you'd genuinely wanted to wipe them out you'd have torn them up. That's not what you did,' he answered.

When we got home, Romil headed for the bedroom, looking sleepy. 'You're going to fall on your face if you walk with your nose buried in your phone,' he said.

He wasn't wrong. The cardboard box filled with my paintings was blocking my way in the dark. The figures in them were gazing at me. I'd said I'd sell them, but I couldn't do it. Had I imprisoned them in the box, or had they imprisoned me? I didn't know.

There was another text from Srijan-da. 'Mallar, what if you see Srijan-da standing at your door tomorrow with your sketchbooks?'

Srijan-da liked to test my vulnerabilities and fears—nothing new about this.

I was about to type, *This door isn't the old one. I've no longer locked myself into the outhouse of my childhood*. Instead, I sent a message about something that needed to be done.

Two days later, a small truck came up to the house. The courier. I put the box of paintings in the back of the truck.

'Take them carefully, they're going to Chennai.'

In my head, I thanked Srijan-da for taking on the weight of all these memories on himself—the flower pots, the sketchbooks and now this box of paintings. I felt unburdened. The load was not as much for him as it was for me, or so I felt. I had a sudden thought. I told the driver, 'Can you unlock the back? I forgot something important.'

Looking annoyed, the driver opened the door. I picked out one of the paintings. *Let a single memory remain*, I reflected, *in the process of unburdening myself, let me not become utterly weightless*. The truck and the boxes left. Back home there was a white patch on the floor where the box had stood. Just like the clean patch left in the dust when a piece of furniture is moved after a long time. I swept away the bare spot with a broom.

Opening my drawer, I found some empty space on one side. Tuhin's sketch was there too. I put the acrylic next to it. I was hoping neither of them would ever have to be retrieved.

In the darkness of night, I saw Romil sleeping peacefully in bed. I was sunk in thought as usual: *You know where I went*

*wrong, Romil? In spending so many years on this effort to complete
an unfinished story. I kept cutting up and then putting together the
same story in various ways, thinking it would become an epic. It
never occurred to me that I could write everything anew.*

I gazed at Romil's calm face. He knew I did this, and normally I let him sleep—I liked looking at him this way. But today
I ended up waking him up despite telling myself I wouldn't.
Sometimes you have to awaken someone you love to tell them
how much you love them. Or else what you want to say remains
sunk in sleep, lost in silence. I said, 'You know, because I'd
pledged once not to love, I've considered life a state of not
loving—I've never been able to think of it differently.'

In childhood I was afraid to shoulder the responsibility of
waking someone up from sleep. I had decided not to think so
much now. The artist may savour the luxury of the incomplete
story, but the lover's heart gets no succour from it. I could tell
from Romil's expression what he wanted to say but couldn't: *You
woke me up just as I'd fallen asleep to tell me this?*

'OK, Mallar, think of it differently now.'

'I will. Tell me, if I break bottles again, will you gather up the
pieces like you did?'

Romil gazed at me for some time in the half-light and half-
darkness of the bedroom. Then he gripped both my hands in his
tightly.

'No.'

'No?'

Drawing me to himself firmly, Romil said, 'I won't let you break the bottles again. I won't even give you the chance.'

One shouldn't waste the night talking. I don't know if Romil understood, but all I said was, 'If you don't succumb to love in this life, you can protect yourself from a lot of pain. But if you keep protecting yourself from everything, you can't really live this life.'